LOVE
⌇ AND ⌇
FREINDSHIP
(SIC)

LOVE
AND
FREINDSHIP

(SIC)

And Other Delusions

BETH ANDREWS

With apologies to Jane Austen

ROBERT HALE · LONDON

© Beth Andrews 2014
First published in Great Britain 2014

ISBN 978-0-7198-1368-9

Robert Hale Limited
Clerkenwell House
Clerkenwell Green
London EC1R 0HT

www.halebooks.com

2 4 6 8 10 9 7 5 3 1

Typeset in Adobe Caslon Pro
Printed in Great Britain by Berforts Information Press Ltd

PART ONE

(Marianne's Introduction)

The tale that follows is a record of the exploits of a most remarkable woman. I would hesitate even to publish something so intimate and incredible, but I am bound to do so by the express wishes of the authoress herself. I feel, however, that I must first give some explanation of how this manuscript came into my possession.

It began on a rainy evening in Bury St Edmunds. Although that town is generally associated with the signing of the august Magna Carta, my mother and I were employed in something much more frivolous: we were attending a performance of *Lovers' Vows* at the Theatre Royal. The play was entertaining enough for a young lady of one-and-twenty like myself, but it was the company that provided the most interest.

We had been seated for no more than twenty minutes when a genteel commotion in the box directly opposite ours attracted our attention. A woman on the shady side of fifty (about the same age as my mother) entered with some fanfare. She was dressed entirely in black, though not the sombre attire of the recently bereaved. Her gown was worked with silver threads and fluttering feathers, so that what might have looked like a ghostly raven more closely resembled an elegant swan. She was surrounded by at least half a dozen gentlemen in varying degrees of dilapidation, each attending her in the obsequious manner of the devoted *cicisbeo*.

'Who on earth is that, Mama?' I asked, as fascinated as the rest of the audience must have been.

My mother, raising her quizzing glass at the undoubtedly arresting spectacle, gave a snort of supreme contempt.

'That,' she answered, 'is the greatest ninnyhammer in England.'

Even as she spoke, the woman in question turned her head and raised her quizzing glass in our direction. She stared at us for a moment, then gave a great smile and waved enthusiastically at us. To my surprise, my mother did not, as I had fully expected, give her the Cut Direct, but inclined her head slightly in recognition.

'Is she a friend of yours?' I enquired, unable to hide the surprise in my voice.

'An acquaintance from my youth,' she confessed, 'whom I have not had the misfortune to meet these twenty years or more.'

'Misfortune?' I was more curious than ever, but Mama cut short further enquiry by delivering a playful rap upon the back of my hand with her closed fan, and admonishing me to mind the play.

I attempted to do as she asked, but could not refrain from casting surreptitious glances at the box where a much more interesting comedy was being played out, as the mysterious female held court while her admirers fought over every smile and pout she deigned to cast their way. I was determined to discover more about this character as soon as we left the theatre, but in the end there was no need for such effort.

After the play, we pushed and pressed our way through the crowd as they left the building, and were scarcely outside on the pavement when we were waylaid by the very lady I had been observing all evening. She flew up to my mother, her gown glittering and fluttering, and embraced her with all the fervour of a bosom friend.

'My dearest Isabel!' she cried. 'What a joy to find you here tonight.'

My mother's response was not quite icy, but it would be excessively generous to describe it as anything more than lukewarm.

'You are looking very well, Laura,' she said.

Laura seemed to be all arms, eyes and teeth, as she responded.

'Yes, but I am weary to death, fending off unwanted suitors and wallowing in unceasing mourning for my beloved Edward.'

'An arduous life, indeed—especially at our age.'

'Ah! I have always been too painfully sensitive to the afflictions of my friends and myself, as you know, Isabel.'

'Of yourself, certainly.'

If Laura detected the criticism in this remark, she did not show it, but turned her attention to me instead.

'But surely this angelic creature cannot be your daughter,

Marianne,' she exclaimed, adding thoughtfully: 'She takes after her father, no doubt.'

'I am his image in petticoats, so I'm told,' I answered, with a respectful bow.

We were almost at the carriage, and the footman prepared to assist my mother up into it.

'Does your papa wear petticoats?' Laura wondered aloud. 'I had an uncle who did the same. His wife often dressed as an Admiral of the Fleet, I believe.'

'Charming.' Mama turned away as she spoke. 'But I'm afraid we must be off, my dear Laura.'

'Pray stop for a moment,' Laura entreated.

'What is it now?'

The other woman seemed completely insensible of any reluctance on my mother's part to comply with her request. She reached out and took my hand unexpectedly, looking at me with such intensity that I was quite taken aback.

'Dearest Marianne,' she said, giving my hand a painful squeeze, 'I always promised your dear mother that I would someday acquaint her daughter with all the particulars of my many adventures.'

I could hear my mother breathe an audible sigh, apparently resigning us both to our fates.

'I believe,' she said, 'that you did once mention something of the sort. I had quite forgotten.'

'But I have not.' Laura's look of smug satisfaction was a treat to see. 'And that momentous occasion has at last arrived.'

'I should be honoured to hear your story, ma'am,' I replied. What else could I say, after all?

'Come to my house tomorrow, then—at noon.'

Having issued what was more in the nature of a command than a request, she apparently deemed refusal to be impossible, and flitted off to rejoin the gentlemen who had congregated some distance away, watching our conversation with jealous eyes. By then we were safely ensconced in the carriage, and I turned to Mama to ensure that my proposed visit was acceptable to her.

'Go with my blessing, dear child.' She shrugged. 'I make no doubt you will be vastly entertained.'

'You do not mind, then?' Somehow I had gathered that she did not entirely approve of her old friend and was in no mood to encourage the acquaintance.

'On the contrary. It may be just what you need.'

'What do you mean?'

'You have been doubting your decision to marry Tom, have you not?'

I blushed in spite of myself, and caught my lips between my teeth. Mama was ever a downy one, and I had always found it nearly impossible to keep a secret from her.

'Tom is a . . . a good sort of man, to be sure. . . .'

'But you wonder if you might not do better, perhaps?'

'I cannot but question if he is the one for me,' I confessed.

'Is he your True Love, you mean?' Mama chuckled softly. 'Your soulmate?'

'Well. . . .' I could feel the colour in my face deepening.

'Yes, I think Laura may be just the tonic.'

I looked at her curiously.

'Did she marry her soulmate?' I asked.

'She did indeed—God help her!'

'Mama!' Her cynical response startled me in spite of myself.

'Forgive me, my love.' She settled back into her seat as the carriage made the turn to our street. 'When you are my age, you will find that passion, like hope, makes a fine breakfast. Once it cools, though, it is less than useless. One wants something more substantial for supper.'

With such bracing words to comfort me, I arrived at Laura's house the next day with feelings of equal parts curiosity and confusion—a state of mind which her reception did nothing to allay. She was dressed in black, and I quickly learned that no other colour was permitted in her wardrobe. Her mourning was perpetual, even if no longer more than superficial.

She dismissed my expressions of gratitude for her kind attentions with the wave of a hand, tending to the tea tray and insisting that she could do no less to the daughter of her oldest friend.

'How did you and Mama become acquainted?' I asked.

She leaned back on the sofa, closing her eyes in reminiscence.

'When I was a girl of sixteen, your mother was my nearest neighbour in the secluded Vale of Uske.'

'It must have been lonely for you,' I said with genuine sympathy.

'Ah yes!' she agreed. 'In fact, my only other companion was my dear governess, Miss Dickson. I can still recall the last words she ever spoke to me.'

'After all these years?'

'Yes indeed. "Kitty," she said. . . .'

'Kitty?' I was mystified.

'It was her pet name for me,' she explained. 'She always said I had the instincts of a cat.'

'Oh.'

'"Kitty, goodnight t'ye," she said.' She dabbed at her eyes, brushing away quite imaginary tears. 'I could not know then that she would be cruelly taken from me forever that very night.'

'She died so suddenly?' I was touched by such a tragic turn of events.

'She eloped with the butler,' Laura corrected me, quite matter-of-factly.

I only just managed to stifle a laugh before replying, 'My mother's friendship must then have become even more significant to you.'

This abrupt reminder gave her pause and she attempted to pick up the thread of her tale, which was already beginning to unravel.

'Ah yes. Your mother.' She nodded sagely. 'My life had been a cloistered one, but your mother had seen The World.'

'Had she?'

'Indeed.' She leaned closer, as if confiding some great secret. 'In all honesty, your mother never possessed a hundredth part of my beauty nor accomplishments, but she had a great deal of *savoir vivre*.'

'I see.'

'She had spent two years at an exclusive London boarding school, had visited Bath for a fortnight, and supped one evening at Southampton.'

It was an impressive curriculum vitae for a young lady of seventeen, I suppose, and I expressed what I hoped was a suitable degree of astonishment.

'She warned me,' Laura continued, 'to beware the idle dissipations of London, the vain luxuries of Bath, and the stinking fish of Southampton.'

'And what did you say to her in return?' I asked.

'That I should probably never experience the manifold temptations of London or Bath, nor smell the fish of Southampton.'

'Something tells me that you were mistaken.'

I had hardly finished speaking when she all but leaped from the sofa.

'I could not then imagine,' she declaimed dramatically, 'how soon I would quit my humble home for the deceitful pleasures of The World!'

'How did your fortunes change so completely?'

She did not reply directly, but went to a nearby cabinet which she carefully unlocked, removing a neatly bound sheaf of papers. She then presented these to me with great fanfare.

'Here,' she announced, 'is my greatest treasure. I entrust it to your keeping, assured that Isabel's daughter will know what to do with it.'

I was somewhat perturbed by this exaggerated degree of confidence in my abilities, and quite reluctant to accept the mysterious object.

'I really do not feel worthy,' I began, but was immediately forestalled.

'Doubtless there is nobody worthy of this great honour,' she agreed. 'But you will do as well as any other.'

'Thank you, ma'am,' I said, duly chastened.

'This,' she continued, 'is the story of my many adventures, from the age of eighteen, when your mother departed from the Vale of Uske and left me friendless and despairing.'

'I'm sure she had not meant to leave you so,' I tried to reassure her, feeling I must offer some defence of my mother's apparent desertion.

'No matter.' Laura sat down beside me once more, taking my hand and squeezing it painfully. 'The World called her away to her own adventure—though it could not, of course, compare with my own.'

I felt obliged to make some appropriate comment, but was momentarily incapable. At last I stammered out what I hoped would be acceptable.

'Naturally not.'

'Dear child.' She released my hand and looked kindly upon me, so I assumed that my words were what she had wanted to hear. 'When I am gone, I wish you to publish these words. The world should know of my sufferings. It may be that they will inspire other young ladies of noble heart and exalted mind.'

'Anything is possible,' said I.

'Would you read it to me?' she asked suddenly, as though the idea had just occurred to her—though I did not doubt that this had been her intention from the beginning of our conversation.

'I can hardly read it all today,' I protested, looking at the considerable number of pages before me.

'No, no,' she agreed. 'You must visit me again. We will enjoy a chapter or two each time.'

It was a daunting prospect, but I acquiesced, if only from curiosity as to the kind of life this unusual woman had led.

So we settled down and I moved to a more comfortable chair, while she stretched out on the sofa to enjoy a period of what surely must have been supreme self-gratification in hearing her exploits recounted by someone other than herself.

What follows is essentially the text which I began to peruse that afternoon and which I later submitted to a publisher in Edinburgh at the request of my supine auditor. Only minimal changes in grammar, and the necessary divisions of some episodes, have been made to the original.

PART TWO

LAURA'S MANUSCRIPT

Chapter One

Many and varied are the afflictions of my life, and I can only hope that the fortitude with which I have borne them may prove a useful lesson for those who face their own trials and tribulations.

My father was a native of Ireland and an inhabitant of Wales. My mother was the illegitimate daughter of a Scots peer by an Italian coloratura soprano. I was born in Spain and received my education at a remote convent in the south of France.

When I reached my eighteenth year, I was recalled by my parents to my paternal home in Wales. Our house was a large one, without being precisely a mansion, and was situated in one of the most romantic parts of the Vale of Uske, ensconced among lush green hills where the sun shone like a golden haze in the mist-shrouded mornings.

I was a paragon of beauty and grace, but these were the

least of my many perfections. I was mistress of every feminine accomplishment, supreme in every art. At the convent, my progress always exceeded the expectation of my teachers, whom I soon surpassed. My proficiency was wonderful, and in my mind every virtue, every good quality, and every noble sentiment was united.

If any fault could be found in me, it was only an excess of humility and a tendency to forget my own perfections. My looks may be faded now, along with my accomplishments: I can neither sing so well nor dance so gracefully as I once did, and have entirely forgotten the minuet now that I have learned to waltz. Nevertheless, at eighteen, I was absolutely incomparable.

My perfections were all quite wasted in the wilderness of Uske, however, for the only person of consequence in our neighbourhood was Isabel, who was already nineteen, practically on the shelf, and eager to accept the first decent proposal of marriage which might come her way, since her parents had left her in indigent circumstances.

At last, to the astonishment of all, Isabel did indeed receive a proposal of marriage and abandoned her friend to find what happiness she might on the distant shores of Ireland. It seemed that I was doomed to waste my youth and beauty alone in a remote residence on the pockmarked posterior of Wales. Such, however, was not the case.

Chapter Two

One evening in December, my father, my mother and I had arranged ourselves in a picturesque tableau around our fireside in the drawing room. I was entertaining myself with Defoe's *Journal of the Plague Year,* while my father puffed contentedly on his pipe and my mother sat studiously embroidering something of no significance whatsoever. The fire was warm and cheerful, while outside a steady rain—not unusual in that part of the country—fell with unwearied persistence.

Our domestic peace and harmony was suddenly shattered by a loud knocking at the front door, which was situated some ten feet from where we sat.

'What noise is that?' my father asked of nobody in particular.

'It sounds like a rapping at the door,' I cried.

Papa took a great puff at his pipe.

'It certainly appears to proceed from some uncommon violence against our unoffending door.'

'I cannot help thinking that it must be somebody who seeks admittance.' I nodded in agreement.

'That is a definite possibility,' he conceded, 'though by no means a certainty.'

As he spoke, the knocking resumed, much louder and more insistent than before.

'The servants are out,' my mother said, plying her needle with increased urgency. 'Whatever shall we do?'

'Should we perhaps go and see who it is?' I asked,

closing my book.

'An excellent idea,' my father replied, beaming upon me.

'Should we go now?' my mother suggested hesitantly.

'With all possible speed,' said I, settling back in my chair.

At that very moment, there was the sound of footsteps approaching, and a moment later, Mary, the parlourmaid, appeared. She was just in time, for the knocking resumed with unprecedented force.

'The servants have returned,' my father said. 'Here is Mary come to get the door.'

'I am glad to hear it,' my mother sighed in relief, 'for I long to know who it is.'

Mary opened the door and peered out into the dark and inclement night. Just as quickly, she closed it again and turned to inform us that that there was a young gentleman and his servant standing outside in the rain. They appeared to have lost their way, were very cold, and begged leave to warm themselves by our fire.

'A young gentleman!' I exclaimed, immediately intrigued. 'You must admit them, Papa.'

'Have you any objection, my dear?' my father enquired of my mother.

'None in the world.'

Mary opened the door once more, not waiting for further instructions, and through the doorway stepped the most beautiful and amiable young man I had ever beheld. My natural sensibility had already been greatly affected by the dramatic situation of the unfortunate stranger; and as soon as I laid eyes on his angelic countenance, I knew that the happiness or misery of my future life must depend entirely upon him.

We all rose in unison, transfixed by this tall, handsome man, romantically attired in a wide-brimmed hat and mysterious-looking cloak.

'Good evening, sir,' my father said.

'Forgive this intrusion.' The stranger bowed formally. 'I saw the light from your cottage and came hither seeking a refuge from the storm.'

'Pray come in, sir.' I stepped forward to greet him at once. 'You are most welcome in our quiet retreat.'

'But who are you?' my father asked. 'And how do you come to be in this remote spot?'

'My family name is Lindsay.' The stranger looked around as if expecting someone to jump out at him from behind the nearby curtain. 'But I'm afraid that I am forced to conceal it from you, and will call myself Talbot.'

'As you please.' Papa shrugged.

'As to how I came here, I have quarrelled with my father, a wealthy baronet whose only concern is to enlarge his already vast estate.'

'A vile wretch he must be!' I exclaimed. 'It hardly seems possible that such a man could be the father of one so noble as yourself.'

'It is puzzling, certainly,' he agreed. 'But I knew that I could depend upon your sympathy and support, and so did not hesitate to reveal so much to such good friends.'

I inched ever closer, as he continued to elaborate on his original statement. He related how his father, Sir Sidney, had confronted his only son and heir in their palatial mansion. Sir Sidney demanded to know whether Edward (the name of our mysterious guest) intended to marry their visitor, Lady Dorothea.

'Marry Lady Dorothea!' Edward cried. 'Never, sir!'

'You seemed much attracted to her,' Sir Sidney returned.

'She is lovely and engaging, and I prefer no woman to her.'

'Then why, in heaven's name, do you object to the match?' his father demanded, becoming increasingly impatient.

'Lady Dorothea is wealthy and titled. What romance can there be in such a connection?'

'Romance! Have you been reading stupid novels again?'

Edward dismissed this ignorant comment.

'More damning than her title, however, is your promotion of the match. A young man who complies with his father's wishes is unfit to be a hero. Never shall I be accused of such a paltry action!'

His stirring narrative aroused my admiration as nothing had ever done before. I clasped my hands together in an ecstasy of ardent passion.

'Noble Edward!' I could not refrain from saying. 'You have done just as you should.'

He inclined his head slightly, accepting the compliment as his due.

'I fled my father's house, intending to seek refuge with my aunt in Middlesex,' he added. 'Yet this vale, I find, is in South Wales.'

'A minor miscalculation in geography,' my father acknowledged.

Suddenly Edward took my small, frail hand in his, firmly but tenderly, and raised it to his lips quite in the grand manner.

'And now, my dear Laura,' he asked, his eyes ablaze as he looked into mine, 'when may I receive the reward for all the sufferings I have endured?'

'What?' I was too giddy to conceive his meaning.

'When will you reward me with yourself?'

I did not hesitate another moment, but immediately replied, 'This very instant, my dearest Edward!'

'I shall perform the ceremony myself,' Papa announced, beaming.

Edward stared at him, all astonishment.

'Are you an ordained minister, then?' he enquired.

'As to that,' my father gave a slight cough, 'I cannot say that I am ordained. But is such a technicality to stand in the way of True Love?'

'No. Never,' I answered emphatically.

'My father originally intended me for the church, and I have attended many a service on a Sunday morning.'

'That is good enough for me!' I said.

'Me too,' Edward echoed.

'And once we are wed,' I assured him, 'we may yet seek out your aunt—our aunt, I may say—in Middlesex.'

'If not Middlesex,' he said, giving my hand a squeeze, 'perhaps Sussex or Wessex—or some other sex.'

'We are of one mind, as ever, my love.'

The hour that followed seemed to pass in a golden haze, which yet remains indelibly etched upon my memory. My mother placed a floral wreath upon my brow. Then, as we stood before my father, Edward placed a ring upon my finger and I saw my mother wipe a tear from her eye with a handkerchief.

The rain cleared as if by magic, and Edward and I mounted his horse and galloped away, while my parents stood at the door of their dwelling, waving a happy farewell. Edward's manservant I never saw again, and assumed that Mary had kept him for herself.

Chapter Three

We took a somewhat circuitous route to the home of Edward's Aunt Philippa, eventually arriving in Middlesex more than a week later. Philippa was surprised by our unexpected arrival, but monstrous kind and accommodating.

Unfortunately, it transpired that Augusta was also visiting her at that time. Readers may not be aware of the fact (since I have quite forgotten to mention it) that my beloved Edward had a sister whose name was Augusta and who, along with her father, had promoted Edward's match to Lady Dorothea.

Augusta was a most cold-hearted, reserved young woman who behaved towards me in an abominable way. She should have perceived at once that I was a most superior person, and yet her arms were not opened to receive me to her heart, though my own were extended to press her to mine. Her demeanour was not cordial, nor her language at all affectionate. Indeed, she wasted little time in quitting the room and requesting a private conference with her brother.

Feeling the need to know what their discussion entailed, I stationed myself as close to the door as possible. Some might call this eavesdropping, but those conversing in the next room should really have been more cautious if they did not want their words—which were not exactly whispered, in any case—to be overheard. After all, the door of the drawing room was not locked, and was even slightly ajar—at least it was after I had ever so gently turned the handle and inched it open.

They were having as fine an argument as two siblings ever enjoyed. Peering through the slit between door and frame, I could perceive them standing close together in the very centre of the room, and it soon became apparent that much of their argument was about his marriage to me.

'Do you think,' Augusta demanded icily, 'that our father will ever be reconciled to this imprudent connection, Edward?'

'What should my father's opinion matter to me?' her brother responded haughtily. 'Have you ever in your life known me to follow his advice in anything?'

'Now that you mention it, I have not.'

'Not since I was five years old have I ever had any thought of my father's happiness.'

'Then how do you expect him to assist in your support?'

I watched as Edward drew himself up and looked down at his sister with supreme contempt.

'Never,' he said, 'would I demean myself by applying to him for aid. Besides, what support should Laura and I require? What do we need but each other?'

'A little food and drink might be welcome now and then,' Augusta answered drily.

'Food and drink!' Edward's voice dripped with disdain. 'Can your vulgar mind conceive of no other support for an exalted sensibility?'

'Clearly my sensibility is not as exalted as yours.' She shrugged. 'I cannot dismiss my digestion so easily.'

'I pity you, sister.'

Augusta put her hands up to his shoulders, as though about to shake him. However, she refrained, and when she spoke her voice was surprisingly calm.

'Do you even know if this girl—this stranger—possesses any of the qualities you wish for in a wife?'

'I ask for no more in my wife than she will find in me: perfection.'

'Edward, tell me plainly how you intend to support yourself and your bride.' She shook her head, apparently bewildered by his attitude. 'You have no profession, no connections of any material advantage to you.'

His next words roused my enraptured soul like a trumpet call!

'Augusta,' he enquired, 'have you never felt the pleasing pangs of love? Can you not conceive the joy of living in poverty and distress with the object of your deepest desire?'

'That is a joy which I can well do without,' she snapped.

At this point they were interrupted by the arrival, through the opposite door to mine, of Sir Sidney himself. He strode forward, approaching them quickly. It was painfully clear that he was an angry man.

'Papa!' Edward exclaimed in some consternation.

'Can what I have heard be true?' Sir Sidney demanded.

'That your son is out of his senses?' Augusta queried with deep sarcasm. 'It is but too true.'

'Say no more, either of you!' Edward cried out, raising an arm before his face, as if to ward off a fatal blow. 'I know your cruel and vicious designs.'

'Do you, indeed?' His father's fury seemed only to increase at this.

'You mean to reproach me for wedding my Laura without your consent!' He struck an attitude.

'Without a great deal of thought, either.'

'Well, I glory in my actions. It is my greatest boast that I have thwarted my father's designs.'

'I see that you are mad.'

'With the madness of true love!' he declared. 'And nothing but death will ever separate me from my beloved.'

With these words, he rushed towards the door where I was watching, his strides so swift that he had opened it before I could move. As a consequence, the door handle struck a stunning blow against my temple. Before I could do more than utter a quick gasp of pain, however, Edward had grabbed me by the arm. Without another word, he dragged me behind him along the hall and out of the front door.

A coach-and-four was drawn up in front of the house with the driver still waiting on the box. Edward shoved me up into the coach, jumping in behind me and closing the door with a snap.

'The London road!' he shouted to the driver. 'And hurry!'

With a crack of the whip, we were away, leaving a cloud of dust behind us. Huddled against my husband, and nursing a sore head, it took me several minutes to collect my thoughts enough to speak.

'Whose carriage is this, my dearest?' I ventured at length.

'My father's.' His countenance was mutinous, his voice perhaps on the verge of petulance.

'Should we borrow it without his permission?' I asked.

'He has several carriages,' Edward answered reasonably. 'This one will scarcely even be missed. Besides, he deserves it for his cruel treatment of me and my charming Laura.'

How could I argue with that? Instead, I settled back in the well-padded seat, perfectly satisfied that Edward would make all right at last.

'But where shall we fly, my love?' I asked several hours later, when night had drawn on and there seemed no end to our journey.

'I have a most particular friend, Augustus,' he explained, 'whom I have known since my days at Cambridge. He and his wife, Sophia, will be happy to take us in.'

'He must be a very particular friend indeed,' I said.

'Oh, he is,' Edward nodded emphatically. 'Believe me, he is!'

Chapter Four

After an uneventful night, we arrived the next morning at the home of Augustus and Sophia. We were immediately admitted by the butler, who led us down a large hallway towards a room from which emerged the sound of a mournful dirge played upon an antique Irish harp.

The butler stepped forward into the room and the music ceased abruptly.

'Mr and Mrs Edward Lindsay to see you, madam,' the old servant announced.

'Mr and Mrs Edward Lindsay!' Sophia repeated, in some astonishment.

Before she could say more, Edward and I rushed in, unable to contain our joy any longer. We pushed past the butler, almost knocking him down in our haste, and flew to embrace the beautiful harpist.

The three of us twined our arms about each other. Sophia expressed her almost ineffable felicity at seeing Edward again, while Edward in turn made the necessary introductions.

'This,' he said, his arms encompassing our two waists, 'is my wife, the Divine Laura.'

'Who else could it be?' Sophia wondered aloud. 'My dearest Laura, you are all that I ever hoped for in Edward's wife!'

'And you, Sophia, are just as he described you to me: somewhat taller than average.'

I kissed her cheek and she returned the gesture.

'We will be the best of friends!' Sophia cried rapturously.

'We will never again be parted!' I added.

We separated ourselves from Edward and clasped each other's hands as we vowed mutual and eternal fidelity.

'Come,' Sophia entreated me, 'let me unfold to you the most inward secrets of my heart.'

'I will not have a thought or wish hidden from you, love-liest Sophia.'

We had almost forgotten Edward, who was looking about him, frowning in some consternation.

'But where is the Beautiful Augustus?' he asked of my new bosom friend. 'What has become of my companion?'

The words had scarcely escaped from his lips when a willowy blonde youth—the veritable image of Sophia, but perhaps more sylph-like—seemed to float into the room through the French windows which led onto the garden beyond.

'Here I am, Edward,' the youth replied. 'Your own dear Augustus.'

In an instant the two men were in each other's arms. Blue eyes stared soulfully into brown as they closed in a passionate embrace.

'My life! My soul!' Edward cried.

'My adorable angel!' Augustus responded.

They were completely oblivious to me and Sophia as their lips met in a kiss of ardent devotion. Sophia and I, much affected by this display of true and unalloyed friend-ship, sighed softly and each wiped a tear from our eyes.

I must mention that Isabel, dear acquaintance as she is, was not so deeply affected when I described the scene to her at a later date on our journey to Scotland, but more of that anon. Isabel seemed to think that the friendship of our respective husbands was a trifle excessive, and that a little restraint might have been more acceptable. How it can be possible for love to be excessive, I do not understand; and as for restraint, it is a word repulsive to anyone of true sensibility. To artificially control and deliberately inhibit one's feelings is abhorrent to me, and I was most distressed to find Isabel so insensible on this matter.

How could I possibly object to the many hours my husband spent alone in his bedchamber with his friend, Augustus? Why, I have heard him say that he would break his own back upon a mountain for his friend! How then, could I deny them the expression of emotions so ennobling and fulfilling to them both? And besides, Sophia and I were as happily employed in mutual protestations of friendship and sharing the most intimate details of our lives for each other's delectation.

Chapter Five

Alas, our bliss was only too short-lived. As readers might surmise, Augustus and Sophia had eloped in defiance of their parents, and were wed but two months before Edward and I arrived to complete our happy circle. They had no money on which to live, apart from a few hundred pounds which Augustus had purloined from his father's escritoire.

Had he foreseen our arrival, no doubt Augustus would have stol . . . that is, he would have procured more money. The rent for the house and our taste for the finest food and wine were our undoing, for not more than three months after we came there, Edward confessed to me that we were all to pieces financially.

There was no one to whom our friends could apply

for aid, since they had informed all their neighbours that they needed nobody except each other, and would accept no visits from persons less exalted than themselves. They might, of course, have attempted a reconciliation with their families, but would have scorned such an ignoble act as much as they would have blushed at the thought of actually paying their debts.

But for all their courage and their insistence on adhering to their democratic principles, what was their reward? Augustus was arrested and taken to Debtors' Prison! Yes, such is the cruel inhumanity of this world, that they would prosecute someone so beautiful simply because he owed a large sum of money to those who needed it to feed their families.

It is difficult to describe the scene in which the officials of His Majesty's government burst into our previously undisturbed sanctuary to lay their rough and uncouth hands upon Augustus. Sophia and I did what we could, by weeping and wailing and wringing our hands in an agony of exquisitely pained emotion. Still, it was to no avail. They dragged him from our presence, his pitiful pleas for liberty and justice unheeded as he begged for mercy from those who had none.

At last, spent from our frantic exertions on his behalf, Sophia and I both fainted alternately upon a conveniently placed sofa. Edward, meanwhile, exacerbated his nerves by striding up and down the room in an agitated manner, weeping copiously. He was still employed in this happy exercise when Sophia and I awoke simultaneously from our stupor.

Sophia started up at once, crying, 'Gone! Gone! My

beloved Augustus is parted from me forever!'

'No.' Edward stopped his incessant pacing, a look of determination upon his countenance. 'It cannot be! How can I live without my soul?'

'Well, if I can,' Sophia answered him somewhat pettishly, 'I'm sure you can too. He's my husband, after all—not yours.'

Ignoring this waspish remark, I looked up at Edward over my tear-stained handkerchief.

'What shall we do, my dearest?' I asked him, confident that he would know just what was to be done.

'I must go to him,' he said decisively. 'I will stand by his side in his prison cell and lament over his misfortunes.'

'A fine ambition,' Sophia agreed. 'But what about us?'

'You and Laura must remain here and lament with one another, then determine what is best to be done before they turn you out of this house.'

He would have left us at once, but I flung myself upon him in a frenzy of sobs and sighs.

'Farewell!' I cried. 'Edward, my dearest husband, farewell!'

He tore himself from my arms with some difficulty, and in a moment was gone from my sight. Left alone with my beloved Sophia, we clung together once more, our excessive grief so overwhelming that there was nothing to do but collapse once more upon the sofa.

It took several days, but when we had recovered our poise to some extent, we began to consider the matter.

'We must apply to Edward's Aunt Philippa for aid, Laura,' Sophia said, with sudden inspiration.

'Impossible, my dear Sophia,' I replied. 'Philippa has just married a young fortune-hunter who is even now in the process of squandering her last penny.'

'What of your parents, then?' she suggested.

Only then did I recall an event so insignificant that it had quite slipped my mind in all the happiness I had known those past months. I refer to the death of my parents almost as soon as I had left the Vale of Uske with my new husband. It seemed they had been in the midst of celebrating the nuptials of their only daughter when a fatal accident had finished them off. When I related this to my friend, she was all amazement.

'What!' she exclaimed. 'Both dead at once? What could account for such a double calamity?'

'Too much sherry, I'm told—combined with a steep staircase.'

'Oh, fatal combination!'

'Well, so much for seeking help from *them*,' I said philosophically.

'Now you are an orphan.' Sophia's voice grew ever more doleful.

'Yes. And the house we lived in was only rented, and my parents had no money saved. In fact, I am destitute.'

Sophia's face brightened, though not in response to my last statement. It seemed she had come up with yet another brilliant idea.

'What of your childhood friend, Isabel?' she wondered aloud. 'Would she not be eager to help you in this, your hour of need?'

'I do not doubt that she would. But she is recently

married herself—though, sadly, she did not elope—and has moved to a distant part of Ireland.'

Sophia moaned at this, crying, 'Then we are indeed doomed.'

'I will not despair,' I said, rallying. 'We will follow Edward, and join him and Augustus in Newgate Prison.'

'But he has been gone these three days and more. It is too late.'

I stood up and stretched out my hands to her as she sat upon the sofa.

'It is never too late, my dear Sophia.'

'To Newgate, then!' She stood with me and we marched out of the room together.

Chapter Six

Edward had ridden off on the horse belonging to Augustus. Therefore, as luck would have it, the coach we had stolen from his father was waiting outside for us. We travelled through the night and by daybreak were in London.

As our carriage moved slowly through the crowded streets of the great city, we stuck our heads out of the window on each side, bellowing loudly to the pedestrians around us.

'Have you seen my Edward?' I would shriek.

'Have you seen her Edward?' Sophia would echo.

Some of the responses we received were most impertinent, I must admit.

'Forget your Edward, my fine lady,' a red-faced gentleman responded, adding with a suggestive wink, 'I'll introduce you to my little friend: he'll satisfy you, I'm willin' to bet!'

A gaudily dressed young woman, her face well painted, looked up at us in surprise.

'Who the 'ell is Edward?' she demanded.

'He is my husband,' I explained eagerly. 'An angel in human form!'

'I've seen my share of Edwards, right enough,' she said with a laugh. 'Can't say as any of them answered to that description, though.'

'She's barmy, she is,' the red-faced man interjected, which elicited a box on the ear from the young woman.

We rolled on for mile upon mile, with much the same result. Sophia slumped ever deeper into her seat, the picture of abject despair. I could not help but be affected by this.

'How can we ever find Edward in this teeming metropolis?' I asked at last.

'Let me try once more, my dearest friend,' Sophia said in a pitiful attempt to comfort me.

'Very well.' I knew my voice held no conviction, but what harm could it do?

Sophia once again stuck her head out of the window and sung out loudly, 'Have you seen her Edward?'

Scarcely had she spoken when a young woman standing directly beside the carriage and wearing a large plumed hat, gazed directly up into her face. The look she cast at my friend was so full of malice that the blood froze in my veins.

'Sophia!' the woman gasped.

'You!' Sophia responded, quite as aghast.

'Trollop!' the woman shouted at her.

'Slut!' Sophia shouted back, quickly withdrawing once more into the carriage and lowering the blind with a snap.

'Who is that lady, Sophia?' I asked, unable to contain my curiosity.

'Nobody,' Sophia said too quickly. 'Driver, move on!'

The driver obeyed her command, and we were soon out of sight and sound of the mysterious female. I observed, however, that Sophia was still visibly shaken. Under the circumstances, it was impossible, of course, for me to refrain from attempting to extract from my friend some details which might elucidate her extraordinary behaviour.

'What is it, dearest Sophia?' I asked presently. 'What has so distressed you?'

'I cannot bear it any longer!' The words burst from her with a rush like the streaming waters of a breached dyke in Holland. 'I must confess.'

'Confess!' I could not hide my own anxiety at these words. 'What can you confess to me, Sophia? I thought you had revealed to me every secret of your heart, every error of your past.'

Her gaze went in every direction except the one which would bring it into contact with my own. She caught her lip between her milk-white, perfectly even teeth, displaying all the signs of tremendous guilt.

'Not quite *all*,' she whispered at length. 'There is something I have hitherto kept from you.'

'Oh treachery!' I cried, drawing back from her in dismay: she in whom I had placed every confidence, whose heart I thought I knew as intimately as my own—to betray me thus!

'I beg you to forgive me, my Laura. It was, after all, many years ago—three at least—when I was a mere girl of fifteen.'

As it was clear that she was in a state bordering on a nervous collapse, I relented enough to ask her to continue. She hesitated for a moment, no doubt struggling with the enormity of what she was about to disclose.

'The truth is that Augustus is not. . . .' She drew a deep breath and stopped altogether.

'Yes, yes!' I demanded impatiently. 'Augustus is not what?'

I fully expected her to say that her husband was not a descendant of Henry VIII and the rightful heir to the throne of England, as he had several times claimed. In this expectation I was mistaken. The answer, when it came, was a thousand times more shocking than I could have ever conceived.

'Augustus is not the first man I have loved,' she cried. 'Before him there was another!'

I flinched, drawing away from her in horror as if she had dealt me a stunning blow. That any woman should not marry her First Love was a betrayal of our deepest beliefs. That there could even be a Second Love, and that it should lead to marriage, was a thing most depraved and disgusting in my eyes. I felt physically ill and could not speak for full five seconds.

'It is wicked, I know,' Sophia continued, her eyes entreating my understanding, though I scarce knew how to give it. 'But all the girls were mad for Charles Hargrove: including Pamela.'

'Pamela?' I asked, still reeling from her revelation.

'The young woman we encountered just now.'

'She was your rival for his affections?'

Sophia nodded reluctantly in agreement.

'I cannot blame her, I suppose.' She sighed, as the painful memories of her misspent past returned. 'Charles was absolute perfection. His face shone like the noonday sun, with a positively godlike beauty.'

'Great God!' I exclaimed. 'Tell me more.'

For the first time Sophia summoned the courage to face me directly before pouring out her heart in a tale which was at once pathetic and salutary. Charles had been the most sought-after bachelor in the country, heir to a large fortune. His parties were the liveliest in the neighbourhood, the guests almost always being carried home dead drunk.

It seemed that Pamela had been so smitten with Charles Hargrove that she vowed she would stop at nothing to win his affections. She determined to accost him at his home, from which she had been barred by Charles and his family. It was some distance from her own humble dwelling, but she made the journey on foot through the woods in the misty chill of autumn.

'I cannot but applaud her bravery and perseverance,' I said, moved in spite of myself.

'Yes,' Sophia replied shortly. 'She had only to make her way from her father's pigsty to the horse pond near the Hargrove mansion. But there had been poachers in the woods. . . .'

Sophia's voice faded away, the knowledge of what was to come pressed so forcefully upon her mind. Nor could I blame her when she concluded her story.

Wearing a large bonnet tied with a pretty yellow ribbon and trimmed with the best threepenny lace from the village, Pamela set out from her father's pigsty, cheeks and eyes aglow in the frosty morn. Briskly and cheerfully she navigated her way through the woods, which grew increasingly gloomy and ominous as she proceeded. Lost in a golden fog of love, however, poor Pamela was oblivious to the danger on every side. Not until the sound of a sharp snap and a piercing scream shattered the dewy stillness did anyone know the tragedy that had befallen her.

'Charles had set traps against the poachers,' Sophia explained, 'and Pamela stepped blindly into one of them, completely crushing her ankle.'

'Oh, cruel Charles,' I cried, 'to wound the hearts and legs of all the fair!'

Sophia concurred with my assessment.

'I had hoped,' she added wistfully, 'that Pamela would have the decency to perish from her wounds, or perhaps cast herself into the river in a fit of despair.'

'That would have been romantic, would it not?' I agreed, my imagination conjuring up the most agreeable vision of Pamela's body floating down the stream, her hair splayed out in the water like a billowing cloak about her bloated corpse.

'One might have written a poem about it,' I rhapsodized. 'How she flung herself into the river, without hesitation or shiver!'

'Nothing could have been more romantic,' Sophia responded, quite of the same mind. 'But Pamela would have none of it. As you saw today, Peg-leg Pamela lives on.'

I leaned forward, wild with curiosity now.

'And what of Charles? Clearly he did not marry either of you.'

Sophia gave a loud sniff and turned away again.

'Charles married Lady Shelvedore.'

'Who is she?'

'A woman ten years his senior,' she said, 'and with ten times his fortune as well.'

'Is he happy, do you think?' I could not help but ask.

'He is certainly wealthy,' she pointed out. 'For some, that is quite enough, I suppose.'

'He was unworthy of your affections,' I declared, seeing that she was inclined to become melancholy at so much dismal remembrance.

'True.' But she did not seem mollified at the thought. 'And I am much better off with my Augustus. Or at least I was, until he was so cruelly taken from me.'

With these words, she dissolved into a fit of weeping. I attempted to comfort her as well as I could.

'There, there, Sophia,' I said, my arm about her shoulders. 'All will be well when we are in prison. You shall be reunited with your Augustus once more.'

'No, no!' she cried, more agitated and lachrymose than ever. 'I cannot bear it. The sight of my beloved in such cruel confinement would be too much for my feelings. The mere thought of it brings on a spasm.'

I did not like the sound of that, I must admit. Spasms

are most unattractive and unromantic, in my opinion. But I was quite unable to conceive of a way to prevent them.

'If we are not to go to Newgate,' I queried, much perplexed, 'whither shall we go?'

As I spoke, there was such an immediate and complete change in Sophia's countenance that I was more astonished than ever.

'I know!' she announced, her face radiant and exulting.

'Know what?'

'I have a relative in Scotland who I am certain would not hesitate to receive me if we sought his aid.'

'But have you only just remembered this?' I demanded.

'This very minute,' she said, nodding decisively.

'It seems an odd thing to have forgotten so completely.'

She looked somewhat annoyed by this remark, answering pettishly, 'You forgot the death of your parents, after all!'

'I do not see why you should be constantly harping on such a trifle,' I rejoined.

'Shall I direct the coachman to drive us to Scotland?' she enquired, ignoring this.

'It is much too far to travel in this coach, without a change of horses,' I pointed out.

'How shall we get there, then?'

'A hot air balloon might be just the thing!'

We both paused a moment to imagine ourselves drifting through the clouds and wafting gently down to earth like two angels from Heaven!

'Where can we hire such a conveyance?' Sophia asked.

'I have no idea,' I confessed.

'Then why bring it up?'

'It seemed so thoroughly romantic,' I answered, which she immediately understood and accepted.

'We have left London now,' she noted, glancing out of the carriage window.

'At the next town, we will get down and travel Post.'

'An excellent plan.'

Chapter Seven

After several days, we arrived at a village so small that its name quite escapes my memory. Settling ourselves in the commodious parlour, we prepared to await the arrival of the stage, which would not be there until the following morning. In the meantime, Sophia begged a sheet of paper from the landlord and settled down at a convenient table with a freshly sharpened quill to write a letter to her cousin. I stood over her, making comments and suggestions wherever appropriate, until she had finished what I conceive to have been one of the greatest models of the epistolary art ever recorded on paper.

'A most eloquent account of our desolate and melancholy situation,' I remarked as she folded and sealed this missive.

'If this does not move his heart, it must be made of marble.'

'If it is, your words will crack it.'

'Let us send it off at once, else we shall arrive in Scotland before it does.'

While she was speaking, I became aware of a great commotion going on in the courtyard outside: the sound of clattering hooves, coach wheels, barking dogs and braying horses. Moving over to the window, I peered through the dusty pane, craning my neck to see what might be going forward.

'What is it, Laura?' Sophia asked, coming to join me.

'A coroneted coach has just arrived at the inn.'

From our vantage point, we could perceive an elderly gentleman descend and make his way gingerly towards the inn door.

'Who can it be?' Sophia wondered aloud.

'I have never seen him before,' I confessed, trembling with unexpected excitement, 'but my heart instinctively murmurs to me that he is my grandfather!'

'You have a heart murmur?' Sophia was somewhat concerned.

Before I could answer this, we both turned around just as the gentleman entered the room. White-haired and leaning heavily upon a cane, he appeared to be as old as Methuselah. He must, at the very least, have reached his ninetieth year.

'Make way for Lord St Clair!' a liveried footman announced grandly.

To this, however, I paid no heed. Rushing over to him at once, I fell on my knees at his feet and declared, 'Oh my beloved grandpapa! Pray acknowledge me as your own dear granddaughter who has been parted from you these many years.'

He looked as if he were likely to fall over in a faint.

After inspecting me closely, however, he presently said in a weak, raspy voice, 'Lord bless me! You are indeed my granddaughter.'

'Didn't I just say so?'

'Your resemblance to my Laurina and Laurina's daughter, my sweet Claudia, cannot be denied. I acknowledge you as the daughter of one and granddaughter of the other.'

I had no time to express my gratitude at his ready acceptance, for he had directed his attention towards Sophia, who had been watching him with a look of wonder upon her face. As his gaze met hers, his eyes grew round in astonishment.

'Good Heavens! Another granddaughter!' he cried, stepping back a pace and almost falling over a gilt chair directly behind him. 'Your resemblance to the beauteous Matilda, daughter of my Laurina's eldest girl, proclaims it!'

Wasting no more time, Sophia rushed into his arms, which were open not so much to receive her as to steady himself.

'Oh, sir!' Sophia was in an ecstasy. 'When I first beheld you, I knew at once that we were in some manner related, but whether through grandfathers or grandmothers, I could not determine.'

While the two were embracing, a handsome young man who was also staying at the inn entered the room from the opposite end. Upon perceiving him, Lord St Clair released Sophia and threw up his hands in ever-increasing surprise.

'Yet another grandchild!' His voice was becoming quite shrill now. 'What unexpected happiness is this, to discover three of my many descendants in the space of three minutes.'

'Oh, happy day!' the young man said, joining our family gathering.

'You, I am certain, are Philander,' Lord St Clair stated decisively, 'the son of my Laurina's third girl, the amiable Bertha.'

'So I am.'

'But the union of my Laurina's grandchildren is not quite complete,' the old man added, shaking his head gravely. 'One member yet remains: Gustavus.'

While he was talking, I had observed a graceful youth seated at a table just beyond the open doorway, listening intently to all that was transpiring. At these last words, the young man rose up from his chair and stepped boldly into the room.

'And here he is!' the youth announced. 'Here is the Gustavus you desire to see.'

I thought it was the end for our grandfather. He looked in danger of succumbing to an apoplectic fit.

'Can it be true?' he demanded.

'It certainly can,' Gustavus insisted. 'I am the son of Agatha, your Laurina's fourth and youngest daughter.'

'I see that you are!'

'What a fortuitous coincidence,' I commented, surveying this unexpected convocation of relatives. Even Sophia, it seemed, was my own cousin—though we never afterward spoke of it, seeing that we were already spiritual sisters and therefore far more closely connected than by mere blood.

'But tell me,' Lord St Clair asked, looking around him, somewhat fearfully it seemed to me, 'have I any other grandchildren at this inn?'

'None that I am aware of, my lord,' Philander answered.

Heaving a sigh of relief, the old man reached into his coat pocket and pulled out a large wad of banknotes. At this sight, our hearts rose and our eyes lit up in anticipation.

'In that case,' he was saying, 'I will provide for you all without further delay. Here are four banknotes of fifty pounds each.'

We all snatched the notes from his hands eagerly. I seem to recall Gustavus attempting to grab hold of two of them, but the old man was stronger than any of us had imagined—at least where his fortune was concerned.

'Take them, children,' he declared, stuffing the remainder back into his pocket. 'And remember that I have done my duty as a grandfather.'

With unexpected vigour, he turned and beat a hasty retreat to the coach which still waited outside. As he departed somewhat precipitously, I could hear him shouting to his coachman: 'Gregory, get me out of here! Now!'

Sophia and I had nowhere to conceal our new-gotten wealth, except for our ample bosoms, where each of us proceeded to stow our banknote. The two young men concealed theirs beneath their coats, I noticed.

Sophia, meanwhile, was visibly distraught at our grandsire's hasty departure.

'Ignoble grandpapa!' she cried, and immediately swooned, slipping almost noiselessly to the floor.

'Unworthy progenitor!' I added, and followed her example.

Chapter Eight

We must have lain thus for a quarter of an hour or more, until at last we began to revive from our double stupor. With heads spinning and senses disordered, we managed to support each other so that we could both stand up again. I do not recall which of us first noticed a certain something missing from our persons, but it was with a near-simultaneous gasp that we each thrust our hands into our cleavage as the horrified realization dawned upon us.

'The banknotes are gone!' Sophia shrieked.

'So are Philander and Gustavus!' I added, pointing out that we were once more quite alone.

Sophia wore a look of mingled pain and puzzlement.

'Do you think that there might be,' she pondered aloud, 'some connection between the disappearance of our money and of our two cousins as well?'

'A most pertinent connection,' I snapped. 'My dearest Sophia, we have been robbed—and it requires no great logic to determine by whom.'

'Can they have gone very far?'

'That is something which we are about to discover.'

Without further ado, I grabbed her hand and hauled her out through the door into the inn yard. Outside all was a bustle of activity. Spying a young ostler, I called out to him in strident tones.

'Holla, boy! Did you see two young men running away from the inn?'

The boy frowned and asked pointedly, 'Two well-dressed

coves?'

'Yes.'

'That'll be them on the hay wain.' He pointed to the gate leading out into the high road.

'*The Hay Wain* by Constable?' I asked, surprised.

'Not by the constable,' he corrected me. 'By the gate.'

Through the open portal I clearly spied a lumbering cart pulled by two sturdy oxen. The cumbersome vehicle was making its way slowly along the muddy, rutted road which ran by the inn. There was a large, burly man who looked to be a gross farmer of some sort. Seated up behind him were two young gentlemen exquisitely attired in coats and breeches which I well remembered, laughing loudly. No doubt they were congratulating each other on a job well done.

'I see the two vile wretches!' I shouted back at Sophia.

'Can we catch up with them?'

I did not bother to answer this query, for I had already caught a glimpse of another cart of much the same sort, which had stopped before the gate while the driver dismounted to fix the yoke which held his team of oxen. As I watched, the conveyance began to move ahead and the driver returned to his seat.

With my hand still clutching Sophia's, I dashed forward and reached the rear of the cart just as it passed the entrance. Hitching up my skirts, I clambered aboard, then reached back to assist Sophia in following suit. Our perch was somewhat precarious, however, as each bump in the road threatened to dislodge us and leave us sprawling in the mud behind. I pushed myself back into the depths of the cart's hay-strewn bed and motioned Sophia to do the same, which she did. Then, twisting about and leaning over the side, I looked ahead to see whether the first cart, containing our vile relations, was still in sight. It was. In fact, it must have been a mere ten or twelve yards ahead of our own.

'Driver!' I screamed as loudly as I was able. 'Follow that cart!' I thought the man would fall from his seat, so startled was he. He looked around, eyes widening in surprise, but apparently perfectly content to have us as passengers.

'Bless my soul! Wherever did you two young ladies come from?'

'Never mind that!' I chided him. 'We must catch those men ahead of us.'

'No worry about that, miss,' he said placidly. 'We're both bound for Donwell Farm.'

Satisfied that we were now giving chase to our two felons, I ventured to stand up, holding on to one of the wooden railings which formed a barrier on either side, and shook my fist at Gustavus and Philander.

'Restore to us our banknotes, you miscreant hounds!' I demanded loudly.

Both men merely laughed in response to this, and Gustavus actually had the impertinence to make a face at me and stick out his tongue. It was he who responded to my challenge.

'Come and get them, madam!' he cried gleefully.

'You will be sorry for your act of treachery, villains!' Sophia screeched, having positioned herself on the opposing side of the conveyance, likewise supporting herself on the wooden railing.

'Who's going to make us sorry?' Philander flung back at her in derision.

'We will!' I answered him.

'And our husbands!' Sophia added.

'Your husband will soon be dancing at the rope's end!' Gustavus taunted—a remark all the more cutting because it was impossible to refute.

This was too much for poor Sophia, who immediately broke into hysterical weeping. I knelt beside her, attempting to soothe her and stem her convulsions of grief. Then, when I had determined that she was beginning to recover, I rose back up and resumed my ranting.

'When I get my hands on you—' I began, addressing the two men once more.

'What will you do then?' Philander interrupted.

'Murder!'

At this point, Sophia looked up from where she lay sprawled at my feet.

'Have we caught up with them yet?'

'Not yet, dearest,' I replied.

'Damn.'

I looked around me. An elderly dame, with a bundle of sticks for a fire, was trudging along the edge of the road, and presently overtook us, giving us a glance of unabashed curiosity. A little urchin, face smeared with dirt, ran up to the wheel of the cart and, keeping pace with it as we went on, began to interrogate me in the rudest fashion.

'Are you wanting to catch up to those two men up there?' he asked first.

'We will apprehend them, never fear!' I said, undaunted.

'If you get down and run after the cart, you're sure to reach it faster than just sitting here in this one.'

Sophia actually gasped at this scandalous suggestion.

'Run after the cart!' she repeated, eyeing the little fellow with considerable animosity.

'On these dirty, muddy roads?' I continued, scarcely able to conceive such a thing. 'In our best gowns? Impossible!'

'Only think how unfashionable!'

'Think of the shocking inelegance of such an activity.'

'I don't know about that,' the boy admitted. 'But you'll never catch them men like this.'

Sophia waved her hand at him in dismissal, while I addressed him rather more directly.

'Be off with you, impertinent brat!'

Unfortunately, even as I spoke, I could see out of the corner of my eye that Philander and Gustavus had leapt from the cart and were running across a neighbouring field faster than the winner of the Winchester Races.

'Look!' the boy exclaimed, pointing in their direction. 'They're getting away!'

'So they are,' I agreed, none too happily.

'Told you so,' he said smugly.

'All is lost,' Sophia wailed.

'Base, unfeeling cousins!'

'You should've run after them,' the urchin commented, pressing home his point.

I merely hunched up my shoulders and turned away, while Sophia closed her eyes and pretended she had not heard him.

'Children,' she commented to nobody in particular,

'should be seen.'

'But definitely not heard!' I finished her thought.

At that, the boy ran off, and I soon saw him hop onto the cart which our cousins had just abandoned.

'I suppose we had best return to the inn,' I said to Sophia, who reluctantly agreed. Our inheritance, it seemed, was lost forever.

Chapter Nine

Since we had progressed less than a quarter of a mile from the inn, it took us only a few minutes to return there. As we were about to enter the gates, we spied an expensive carriage approaching rapidly on the road. At first we thought it might be Lord St Clair returning with more banknotes. In this, however, we were mistaken. As we approached it, it became obvious that we had never seen this particular carriage before.

A man thrust his head out of the window and addressed us at once.

'I'm after finding my relative,' he said in a pronounced Scottish accent. 'Would either of you two ladies be Sophia?'

It was, of course, Sophia's relative, MacDonald, the very person to whom she had written her letter. He was a tall, well-built gentleman of about forty, but frightfully dour-looking.

'I am Sophia,' my friend announced with genuine joy.

'Get you into my carriage, then.' He opened the door

and reached out an arm to assist her.

'But what of my friend, the beautiful Laura?'

'Your friend?' He frowned.

'More than my friend,' Sophia insisted. 'She is my confidante and the consoler of my many sorrows—and practically a relation, through Lord St Clair.'

'I don't know this St Clair fellow,' MacDonald said. 'But your friend is welcome to join us, since she seems to be as pathetic as yourself.'

We bundled ourselves in the carriage, staring across at the gentleman, who returned our stares with interest.

'Thank God you are come, sir!' Sophia cried. 'Had you my letter?'

I coughed discreetly. 'We never actually sent it, my dear, if you recall.'

'True. True.' She looked at him still more intently. 'How, then, did you find us, sir?'

'I know nothing of any letter. I was visiting your poor parents, who asked me to look in on you and your new husband, to see how you were getting on.'

After learning that she had been cast out of her rented villa, and her husband imprisoned, he set out to find her out of a sense of duty to his family.

'And here you are.' She beamed upon him. Indeed, we were both all smiles, little suspecting what the ultimate result of our rescue would be.

'I am always eager to help any of my relations whenever they are in need.'

'Sir,' I said, 'I see that we have found in you a most tender-hearted and sympathetic friend.'

'Aye,' he said, frowning.

We turned our attention to the passing scenery, when a thought suddenly occurred to Sophia.

'But where are you taking us, sir?'

'To MacDonald Hall, of course: to my home.'

'It sounds very grand,' Sophia commented.

'The very name conjures images of a great stone castle with golden arches at the entrance.'

For the first time our rescuer seemed in danger of smiling. If he did not quite achieve that feat, he relaxed enough to speak a little less harshly.

'It's a comfortable pile, indeed. My daughter is looking forward to meeting you.'

The rest of the journey was tedious and unexciting. The castle, however, when we arrived, was all that the home of the MacDonalds should be, even without the golden arches I had envisaged. The entrance hall was a grand, cave-like room, at the end of which MacDonald's daughter, Janetta, sat beside an enormous stone hearth where a fire blazed cheerfully—the one cheerful note in an otherwise deliciously Gothic interior.

Janetta was a girl of about sixteen, a little short and plump, pretty enough in an unpretentious way. At her feet lay a great shaggy dog, warming himself before the fire; across from her sat an attractive young man a few years her elder.

Janetta rose to her feet, turning eagerly to greet us. Sophia would have rushed to embrace her, but was prevented by the dog, who jumped up at once and began to bark fiercely at us both. Janetta spoke sharply to the animal, who instantly sat down and ceased his noise, though he continued to eye us with a look which was decidedly uninviting.

'Dearest Janetta! We meet at last.' Sophia embraced her with a trifle less passion than usual, as she watched the dog with some misgiving.

'It is good to see you, Cousin Sophia.'

'And this,' Sophia turned to indicate me, standing two paces behind her, 'is my bosom friend, Laura. We have experienced such vicissitudes together as have united our two souls forever.'

'Have you?' Janetta looked quite taken aback, but she recovered quickly and brought forward the young man beside her, adding, 'This is my fiancé, Graham.'

'What!' Sophia cried, but with little enthusiasm.

'Are you soon to be married, then?' I asked.

'This autumn, very likely,' Janetta admitted with a shy smile.

I looked at them both suspiciously. In truth, I could discern no trace of the tender passion in either. There was no wild look in their eyes, no hectic flush upon their cheeks, and no incivility displayed to anyone around them. This was most strange and unaccountable.

'It will be a happy occasion for all,' MacDonald spoke up, with a look of dreadful satisfaction on his face.

'This union has your approval then, sir?' I demanded, wanting to know the worst right away.

'It has been my greatest wish for them since they were children.'

Sophia and I exchanged a look of utter horror at this,

and we knew at once why fate had brought us to this place: to liberate the hapless Janetta from a shameless arranged marriage.

Later that night, closeted together in Sophia's room—which, by the by, was quite the most ornate bedchamber either of us had ever occupied in our lives—we put our heads together to hatch as pretty a plot as was ever conceived. We simply could not allow the chit to wed a man of whom her father approved.

It was not as easy a task as one might imagine. To own the truth, Janetta was not the most promising student in the art of romance. Of course she was very young and ignorant of many important matters, and inclined to be irritatingly prosaic—a trait which she no doubt inherited from her papa. We would do what we were able to remedy these defects, and began our campaign two days later.

Chapter Ten

We determined firstly to interrogate Janetta concerning her relationship with Graham, which (although she did not realize it) was sadly lacking. We were in the great parlour at MacDonald Hall, seated together in three large gilt chairs, arranged in a semi-circle with Janetta at the centre and us on the outer edges, facing her.

'Pray tell us, delightful Janetta,' Sophia began, 'do you truly love Graham?'

'Does he ignite the warmest fires of passion and stir the

depths of devotion in your soul?' I added, the better to elucidate the question.

Janetta blinked and stammered as she replied, 'Well, really, I do not . . . I've never. . . .'

'Ah! Poor child,' Sophia interrupted. 'I see that he does not.'

'You have clearly been coerced into accepting his offer by your mercenary and insensible father.' I nodded sagely.

'No indeed!' Janetta was adamant in her defence. 'Papa would never do such a thing. I like Graham very much. We have been friends since childhood.'

Sophia and I exchanged expressive glances and, in accordance with our prearranged plans, deemed it best to turn the conversation in a slightly different direction.

'Tell me, dear Janetta, what qualities does Graham possess that you most admire?'

'Well . . . he is so very sensible and. . . .'

'Stop!' I cried, aghast. 'Worse you could not say of him.'

Janetta seemed incapable of comprehending this opinion, shaking her head and attempting to understand it, but without much success.

'What do you mean?' she asked at length. 'Should I not wish to marry a man of sense?'

'You should want to marry a man of fire,' I insisted. 'A man of passion and reckless impulse is what you need.'

'Do I?'

'But pray,' Sophia continued, 'what else has Graham to recommend him?'

'He is well-informed and agreeable.'

I dismissed this description with a snort of contempt.

'We do not pretend,' Sophia commented, 'to judge of such trifles as those.'

'We are convinced that Graham has no soul.'

'I thought everyone had a soul,' poor Janetta muttered, but we ignored her attempt at justification.

'Tell me,' I asked, coming to the heart of the matter, 'has he ever read *The Sorrows of Young Werther?*'

Janetta was more mystified than ever, and it was several seconds before she could frame a response.

'I do not suppose that he has ever heard of them. Nor indeed have I.'

At this, Sophia clutched at her chest and I reeled back in my chair, feeling that I might at any moment expire from the shock of it.

'Do you mean to say,' Sophia asked, when she had recovered her poise enough to speak, 'that you have never heard of Goethe?'

'"Goitre"?' Janetta quite misconstrued our meaning. 'Yes, a cousin of mine had an enormous swelling of the throat: quite horrible, it was.'

'No, no!' I cried, almost angry at her obtuseness. 'Not "goitre" but "Goethe". Are you unacquainted with the divine German author?'

'I'm afraid I know nothing of him,' she confessed. 'Should I find him entertaining?'

This crude suggestion was almost too much for my refined sensibilities.

'Goethe entertaining!' I cried, almost in pain.

'I assure you, Janetta,' Sophia attempted to finish my speech, since I was momentarily speechless, 'that Goethe has never written one word which could be considered entertaining.'

'One can scarcely even conceive of such a possibility,' I was finally able to contribute. 'Goethe has never given anyone a moment of pleasure!'

'Except, perhaps, Mrs Goethe,' Sophia interjected slyly.

'I think not.' I refused to relinquish my point.

'But if he is not entertaining,' Janetta insisted, 'why do you expect me to read him? I do not understand.'

I realized that I was speaking to an infant in the ways of love, and must summon all my patience and fortitude.

'Goethe,' I said very slowly, 'is the very essence of romance.'

By now thoroughly confused, Janetta put forward the most hideous suggestion of all: 'Perhaps I should consult my father about this.'

'Foolish child!' Sophia corrected her. 'That is the very last thing you should do.'

'You must learn to cultivate a suitable contempt for the beliefs of your elders, and a most enlightened confidence in your own opinions, however ill-informed.'

'Is this true, Laura?'

'If you wish to be a thoroughly modern young lady,' I said adamantly.

'And you must begin,' Sophia brought us back to the original point, 'by rejecting the unsuitable Graham.'

I took pity on the bewildered girl, patting her on the head like a young, eager puppy.

'Why,' I said sadly, 'the poor man's hair has not the slightest resemblance to auburn.'

'No indeed,' Janetta said, considering the matter. 'It is very true, now I think on it.'

'So you see how impossible it is that you could ever love him.'

'And,' Sophia pressed the point, 'that it is your duty, as a girl of almost sixteen, to disobey your father.'

Janetta nodded, quite cowed now by our barrage of questions and edicts.

'It seems the world is changing,' she said a little wistfully, 'and one dare not let intelligence or virtue keep one from changing with it.'

'Quite so,' Sophia and I agreed in unison, pleased with her quick understanding.

Chapter Eleven

The next day, as we walked in the extensive garden surrounding the castle, we continued to lead her down the path towards her ultimate fate. She still occasionally displayed signs of intransigence and incomprehension, but we worked on her with ferocious diligence until she was wholly converted to our way of thinking.

'Tell me, my dear Janetta,' I began, 'is there not some other man in the neighbourhood for whom you feel the stirring of passion in your loins?'

'What?'

'Laura means to say,' Sophia interpreted, 'that there must be some gentleman of your acquaintance whom you find attractive. Is that not so?'

'No.'

'No!' I veritably screeched, grabbing her arm and almost twisting it in my fervour. 'Think carefully, Janetta. Surely there is some man whose face and form set him apart as the one to whom you can give your heart and hand.'

Janetta shook her head, a little ashamed at being unable to produce the desired answer.

'No,' she said again. 'Nobody.'

'Impossible!' I cried, exasperated.

'Are there any other young men at all living in the surrounding neighbourhood?' Sophia asked more gently.

Janetta paused, her face screwed up in an effort of concentration. At last she was able to produce one name.

'There is Captain M'Kenrie,' she said.

'I knew it!' I carolled triumphantly.

'And is Captain M'Kenrie not handsome?'

'He is well enough, I suppose.' Janetta shrugged, looking somewhat doubtful.

'A paragon, undoubtedly!' I corrected her.

Sophia, meanwhile, was in a euphoric dream, her hands clasped together almost as if in prayer, as she began to rhapsodize over this as yet unseen gentleman.

'A captain.' She sighed soulfully. 'Only imagine him in his uniform . . . so dashing and heroic!'

'Does your heart not beat faster at the mere thought, Janetta?'

'Not noticeably so, no.'

Her dullness could be very irritating at times, but I refused to be defeated.

'Only think of his fine figure!' I commanded her.

'Now that you mention it,' she squeezed the words out with some effort, 'I believe he does have rather a good figure.'

'Of course he has!'

'And a noble heart as well, I'd wager,' Sophia suggested.

'A girl would have to be out of her senses if she were not in love with such a man!'

We had finally worn Janetta down, and she seized on the idea with an almost evangelical zeal.

'She would, wouldn't she?'

'You *are* violently in love with him, are you not, dear Janetta?' Sophia whispered in her ear like the serpent in another famous garden.

For a moment our prize pupil hesitated.

'I would not put it like that,' she ventured slowly. 'I do not think I am a very violent person, after all.'

'But violence is the very essence of love!' Sophia pointed out.

I could see her confidence in our wisdom beginning to waver, and once more leaned towards her, urging her on.

'Come child, do not be shy. You can admit your love to us in all confidence. We are all friends here.'

'I suppose I must be in love with him, then.'

'There, you see!' Sophia said gaily. 'That was not so difficult, was it?'

'I do love him!' Janetta declared, whipping herself up into such a fine frenzy that she almost believed it herself.

'And of course,' I added, 'it stands to reason that he adores you.'

Janetta seemed momentarily to come down from the lofty heights to which she had risen in her imagination.

'Why should you think such a thing?'

'Has he not demonstrated it in a thousand different ways?' I asked.

'I have never known him to do so.'

'You must be mistaken.' Sophia refused to accept her answer.

'Think, Janetta,' I implored her. 'Did he never gaze on you with admiration?'

Sophia, catching the wave of emotion, rode it to the shore of self-deception in a flash.

'Did he never,' she asked Janetta, 'tenderly press your hand, drop an involuntary tear, and leave the room abruptly?'

'Not that I can recall.'

'Try harder, dear,' I said, somewhat drily.

'He always leaves the room when his visit is ended, but never abruptly or without making a bow.'

'Perhaps on those occasions you failed to notice his confusion and despair?'

'Perhaps,' she conceded.

'And I cannot believe,' Sophia said tartly, 'that he could ever do anything so common as making a bow, or that he could ever behave like any ordinary person.'

'He seems ordinary enough to me,' Janetta said sadly.

Chapter Twelve

We said no more at that time. Later that night, however, Sophia and I were lying on her bed, staring up at the richly festooned canopy above us and considering what scheme we might contrive to prevent the terrible catastrophe which we feared might befall the poor misguided girl.

'Janetta must not be allowed to marry Graham,' I declared resolutely.

'If only we could make Captain M'Kenrie aware of her intense passion ... her hopeless devotion,' Sophia suggested.

At her words, I sat bolt upright in bed, light dawning unexpectedly.

'But why not?' I cried, turning towards my companion. 'What should prevent us from doing so?'

Sophia followed my example, sitting up and staring into my eyes in sudden comprehension.

'You mean. . . ?'

'We shall write to the captain ourselves!'

Considering that he who hesitates is lost, we immediately leapt from the bed and dashed into the adjoining sitting room, where stood a good-sized writing desk and all the necessary paraphernalia. I sat down at the desk and picked up a sheet of paper and quill. Then, even as I raised my hand, Sophia interrupted me.

'But wait!' she cried. 'Whom shall we entrust with this missive once it is written?'

'Any one of the servants will do.'

'Might they not inform MacDonald?'

I gasped. She was right, of course. The servants would no doubt suspect that something was amiss and inform their master at once.

'Besides,' Sophia continued, 'what if he cannot read? One can never be sure of anyone below the rank of general, I think.'

'True, true,' I agreed.

'What are we to do, then?'

'There is but one course open to us.' I stood up, squaring my shoulders. 'We must go to Captain M'Kenrie and plead Janetta's cause to him in person.'

'A delightful notion!' Sophia was persuaded at once.

On this note, we returned to bed and a long, refreshing sleep. The next morning we left the Hall early, making our way into town and enquiring where the man we sought might be lodging. In such a small hamlet, it did not take much searching before we arrived at his door. It seemed he shared rooms with a fellow officer. Mercifully, the man had spent the night with a doxy on the other side of town and was passed out in a drunken stupor so that M'Kenrie was practically alone when we knocked energetically upon his door.

It was some minutes before he answered, and we heard a deal of scuffling and muttered words from the other side. At length the door opened a few inches and a much-dishevelled gentleman stared out at us. He was tall and not ill-favoured, but clearly greatly surprised to be confronted by two strange women at such an hour of the day.

'What's all this, then?' he demanded.

'Sir,' I began, pushing past him before he knew what I was about, 'we come on an urgent mission, which much concerns your future happiness.'

By this time, Sophia had also edged her way past him. We now stood in the centre of the small room, while he leaned against the door, which had closed behind us.

'What nonsense are you talking?'

I had taken the liberty of rehearsing a speech while we made our way to his domicile, and now, placing my hand over my heart, I opened my lips and intoned: 'Oh, happy lover of the young and beautiful Janetta.'

'Who the hell is Janetta?'

By this time, M'Kenrie's roommate had roused himself from his semi-comatose condition and added his mite to our little scene.

'Don't be daft, lad,' he chided his friend. 'You must remember the daughter of old MacDonald?'

'From the farm?' M'Kenrie asked, still quite befuddled.

'From MacDonald Hall, you great loon!'

M'Kenrie perked up at this, and seemed much more sobre himself.

'D'you mean the young heiress?' he asked.

'The same,' I answered at once.

'But I hardly know the girl!' he protested.

'According to these two,' his friend said, 'you're her lover!'

I immediately spied my opportunity to continue my speech.

'You who possess Janetta's heart,' I cried, dabbing at my eyes with a moist handkerchief for full effect, 'why do you delay so cruelly the confession of your attachment, when her hand is destined to another?'

'Delay what?' He seemed more at sea than ever.

'The confession of your attachment,' Sophia instructed him. 'Keep up, sir, for Heaven's sake!'

'A few short weeks will put an end to every hope you entertain, by uniting this unfortunate victim of her father's cruelty to the detestable Graham!' At this, I hissed dramatically, which startled both men. 'I beg you to reveal your dark desire and persuade her into a secret union which will secure the happiness of you both.'

'There you have it!' the friend declared at the conclusion of my speech. 'She's all a-twitter over you, if what they're saying is true.'

'I can hardly believe it.'

'What are you going to do about it?' Sophia asked, growing impatient.

'I'm going to MacDonald Hall as fast as I can,' he replied without hesitation. 'I'm not such a fool as to let a real, live heiress slip through my fingers!'

He paused only long enough to shave and wash, and prepared to adorn himself in his dress uniform, which we considered would be most effective. We informed him that we would return to MacDonald Hall ahead of him and have Janetta ready to meet him when he arrived.

We made sure that Janetta's father was off hunting before we brought her down, quite unsuspecting, to continue our previously arranged time of reading. I had a volume of *Clarissa Harlowe* before me, while Sophia perused a worn copy of *The Monk* and Janetta struggled to make sense of *The Sorrows of Young Werther.*

Suddenly M'Kenrie burst into the room. He was quite a spectacle, as even I was forced to admit: wet from head to toe, his white linen shirt clinging to his manly form like a second skin while he held his scarlet coat in his left hand.

'Captain M'Kenrie!' Janetta cried, in shocked disbelief. 'What are you doing here? And why are you all wet?'

'Clearly he has been swimming in the loch, in order to cool his overwhelming passion for you!' Sophia cried, quite enraptured.

'Actually,' MacDonald said apologetically, 'I slipped and fell into a horse trough.'

There was an awkward silence, while I frantically made signs to M'Kenrie behind Janetta's back. He seemed at length to grasp my meaning, and strode forward, falling on one knee before the girl.

'My dearest . . . um . . . Jemima.'

'Janetta,' I corrected him.

'My dearest Janetta,' he tried again. 'Only my modesty has thus far kept me from declaring the depth of my passion for you.'

'Passion!' Janetta looked as if she wanted to run, but I held her arm firmly in my grasp.

'Once I knew of your feelings for me,' M'Kenrie went on, warming to his theme now, 'I flew here on the wings of love. If you will but consent to wed one so far beneath you, then take my hand—for you already own my heart!'

Janetta looked from me to Sophia, not knowing how to respond to such words.

'What shall I do?' she begged.

'Think, Janetta!' Sophia urged her. 'Think of Werther.'

'I should shoot myself?' Janetta cried, horrified.

'No, no!' I said.

'Should I shoot M'Kenrie, then?'

'It's your father who'll be doin' the shootin', m'dear,' M'Kenrie answered. 'But I'm thinkin' he'd best start with these two.'

Sophia and I were quite taken aback by this remark, since he clearly indicated the two of us.

'What do you mean?' I demanded, eyeing him with rather less approbation.

'Only that you're as much a part of this as any of us.' He shrugged. 'This is as much your affair as mine and Jemima's.'

'Janetta's.' Sophia and I corrected him in unison.

Janetta just stood there like a lump, looking mighty bewildered.

'For Heaven's sake, girl,' I said in some exasperation, 'kiss the man!'

M'Kenrie took the hint, even if she did not. Rising from his knee, he grabbed her in his arms with some ferocity and bestowed a passionate kiss upon her unprepared lips.

'That's better!' I said with approval.

'It certainly is!' Janetta agreed wholeheartedly.

'Not bad, I must admit.' The captain appeared pleasantly surprised.

'What shall we do now?' Janetta enquired, looking up at the man who could now officially be termed her lover.

'Your father will never give his consent to our union,' he said flatly.

'I should hope not!' Sophia commented.

'You must elope,' I pointed out what seemed absurdly obvious. 'There is no other option.'

'Elope!' Janetta looked terrified. 'To Gretna Green?'

At last our protégée had conceived a plan which was all I could have wished for. I could not refrain from giving her a congratulatory hug.

'A capital notion!' I cried. 'Nothing could be so frightfully romantic.'

'Nothing could be so frightfully expensive, and at a considerable distance from MacDonald Hall,' Captain M'Kenrie added.

'Nor is it really necessary,' Janetta put in. 'One only goes to Gretna if one is eloping from England, since it is so near the border.'

'Still,' I persisted, 'there is something about Gretna. No other town will do, I'm afraid.'

'Besides,' Sophia added rapturously, 'what does distance matter to the heart?'

'It's not the heart, but the purse that's the problem.'

'You have not enough money?' I asked in some consternation.

M'Kenrie cleared his throat and looked somewhat sheepish.

'There are ... debts ... that must be paid, ma'am. A matter of honour, you understand.'

'Gaming debts, you mean?' Janetta's eyes seemed likely to shoot out of their sockets like two bullets. 'Are you a gamester, sir?'

He seemed to recognize that this revelation did nothing to advance his cause with the young lady, and hastened to undo the damage as speedily as possible.

'That is all in the past, my sweet.' He placed his arm around her and looked soulfully into her eyes. 'From the moment I set eyes on you, I have been a changed man.'

Amazingly, this heartfelt speech did not seem to have much of an effect on the girl. She looked decidedly unconvinced.

'Never mind,' Sophia interrupted them. 'I shall give you the money for the journey as a wedding present.'

'Where did you get the money from, cousin?' Janetta was all astonishment. 'I thought you were quite destitute.'

Sophia never batted an eyelash.

'I extracted it from the strongbox your father keeps in the drawer of his private desk.'

'You stole it from Papa!' Janetta gasped.

'*Stealing* is a word which has such negative connotations,' Sophia protested. 'I find your use of it strongly offensive to myself.'

'Besides,' I added, 'MacDonald deserves no better. Only think of his dastardly treatment of you and your gallant lover.'

'But he has done nothing to either of us,' Janetta pointed out with a return to her distressingly matter-of-fact attitude. 'Indeed, he is perfectly ignorant of our attachment—as I was myself until just a few days ago.'

'Why worry your head with such trifling matters?' Sophia wondered aloud, adding, 'In any case, your father *will* treat you both abominably once he learns of your scandalous elopement.'

'There can be no doubt of that,' I seconded.

'But stealing,' Janetta stubbornly insisted, 'cannot be right.'

She crossed her arms, and it began to look as though she were going to be alarmingly stubborn on this point. I knew that I must try to make her understand the ways of the world, of which she was clearly much ignorant.

'Right and wrong, good and evil,' I said gently, as to a child, 'are foolish distinctions which great souls like ourselves leave to those who are less enlightened.'

'If right and wrong are essentially meaningless,' she answered pertly, 'then it stands to reason that you cannot possibly condemn Papa's treatment of myself—or anybody's treatment of anyone! It is all relative.'

The sudden intrusion of logic into the conversation overset me momentarily, but I recovered quickly.

'Of course, certain actions are more . . . acceptable . . . than others, when done by certain persons who are more . . . enlightened. . . .'

'This is nonsense!' Janetta interrupted me quite rudely. 'Has all you have told me been equally silly?'

'Do not fling logic at us, my dear Janetta,' Sophia said, painfully stung by her baseless accusations. 'Some things are above reason, after all.'

'And some are beneath contempt,' M'Kenrie commented.

'I'm sure I don't know what you mean, sir,' Sophia replied.

'Just give me the money, ma'am.' The captain held out his hand, his eyes hard and cold. 'I'll take care of the rest.'

'I don't know about this,' Janetta said, stepping back, and looking almost as if she were about to run away.

'But I do!'

These words were spoken by M'Kenrie; and, to give him credit, he wasted no time in demonstrating why she should indeed elope with him. In a flash, she was in his arms and being thoroughly kissed once more, with a great deal of fondling and mauling besides. When he finally raised his head, Janetta was so overcome by emotion that she seemed about to swoon. I took this as the perfect time to whisk her away.

'Do hurry, Sophia,' I urged my friend. 'We do not want MacDonald to apprehend them before they have even reached the high road.'

'He'll take the high road,' M'Kenrie smiled. 'But I'll take the low road.'

With that, he grabbed the money in one hand and Janetta's wrist in the other, practically dragging her out of the door with him. She looked back at us for a moment, helpless and with an air of indecision and regret. Then they were both gone from our sight, disappearing down the front steps towards the waiting carriage.

Chapter Thirteen

Sophia and I turned and went back into the house with a sigh of satisfaction.

'We have set those two on the path to perfect happiness,' she said, 'but I am quite exhausted from all this philanthropy.'

'You really should lie down, my dearest,' I said with tender consideration.

We had just left the great hall and turned into the passage which led to our bedchambers, when Sophia stopped suddenly.

'Oh, Heavens!' she cried. 'I have just remembered something.'

'What is it?'

'The banknotes which I gave to M'Kenrie were my last.'

'You must certainly replenish your supply, then.'

She nodded in agreement, then turned and went another way along the corridor.

'MacDonald's study,' she reminded me, 'is this way.'

We opened the door and stepped into a dark, book-lined room with heavy, carved mahogany furniture, the whole dominated by a massive desk with a superfluity of drawers. Sophia went immediately to the correct one and withdrew a small box which was heavily bound in brass and locked securely.

Withdrawing a hatpin from her elaborate chapeau, she went to work at once, and it was clear that she was no novice in this particular art. Glancing around the room, meanwhile, I happened to spy a small Dresden figurine on a shelf, which was very pretty. I slipped it into my reticule and leaned over to observe Sophia's abilities.

We were too involved to notice that the door—which we had carelessly left ajar—had opened to its fullest extent. It must have been several seconds before a movement to my left caused me to raise my head and look towards the entrance.

'MacDonald!' I cried, causing Sophia to drop everything just as the lock sprang open, scattering the contents on her lap.

It was the master of the Hall himself, glaring at us with an extremely grim expression on his face.

'Do you not know, sir,' Sophia confronted him at once, 'that it is not at all good manners to insolently break in upon a lady in her retirement?'

MacDonald chose to ignore her lesson in etiquette.

'Pray tell me, ma'am, what are you doing in my private chamber with my strongbox in your hands?'

'I conceive that to be none of your business, sir.' Sophia treated him to a look of haughty disdain.

'I've noticed money missing on several occasions recently,' he persisted, his stare more piercing than ever. 'But however mentally deranged you might be, I could not bring myself to believe that you were no more than a common thief.'

'How dare you refer to me as "common"!' Sophia cried, rising from her seat in righteous indignation, and dislodging a banknote which dangled jauntily from the open strongbox.

'I beg pardon, strumpet,' MacDonald shot back.

I could not stand idly by while my friend was being subjected to such Turkish treatment by this ruffian. I sprang to her defence at once.

'You little know your cousin,' I said, giving him stare for stare, 'if you can accuse her of an act of which the merest idea must make her blush.'

'Aye,' he said. 'And if she did blush, it could only be from shame.'

'Base miscreant!' Sophia shouted at him. 'To attempt to sully my spotless reputation!'

'Well then, madam.' MacDonald was dangerously calm. 'If you were not robbing me, pray tell me what you were doing.'

I thought for a moment, casting about in my mind for a suitable explanation.

'She was gracefully purloining a few pounds whose loss someone in your position would scarcely even notice—and which should have been placed at her disposal, in any case, as your honoured guest.'

MacDonald folded his arms across his chest and raised a brow at this.

'In that case,' he said through clenched teeth, 'I will not throw you out of my house. I shall merely assist you in departing my residence with all possible speed: something which I should have done some weeks ago!'

I could see that Sophia was wounded to the heart by his perfidious behaviour.

'And when I think,' she said, lips trembling, 'of the singular service which we have lately rendered to your lovely daughter, I do not know how you have the heart to accuse either of us.'

'Singular service?' His brows drew together, and his voice rumbled like distant thunder.

Then the story of our Herculean labours on Janetta's behalf came out, mingled with many a tear and sigh as we lingered on the difficulties we had encountered with his headstrong daughter.

Naturally, we did not expect him to approve his

daughter's match, but I still consider his response to have been somewhat excessive.

'You have thrown my daughter into the arms of an unprincipled fortune-hunter,' he exclaimed at the conclusion of our touching narrative. 'Thanks to you, she will be ruined forever.'

'We merely performed the duty of true friendship,' Sophia corrected him.

'I am sure,' his lip curled as he spoke, 'that Elizabeth Tudor never did more for Mary Queen of Scots!'

'Thank you, sir,' I said, speaking for us both.

'Get out,' was all his answer.

This was followed by a deplorable contravention of traditional Scottish hospitality, in which he dragged us, kicking and screaming, out of the house by our hair. We were cast down the front steps like so much rubbish, and a servant subsequently threw our belongings out of an upstairs window onto the lawn, for us to collect at our leisure.

Even as we tumbled down the stone stairway, I could hear MacDonald's voice threatening to set Darcy upon us. Recalling that this was the name of the ferocious hound which had so frightened Sophia on our first night at MacDonald Hall, we wasted no time on grace and decorum, but ran as fast as we could down the drive.

Our one bit of good fortune was that Sophia very soon discovered in the lining of her coat, where it lay on the freshly cut grass, one of the purloined banknotes which she had squirrelled away the week before and quite forgotten.

Clutching our satchels, containing what remained of our belongings, we trudged past the gates for the last time, whiling away the minutes by berating MacDonald for his contemptible treatment, his pernicious ingratitude, and his crudity which had so distressed our exalted minds. Indeed, that is the one defect of possessing an exalted mind: it is too easily distressed to be long comfortable.

We had walked just over a mile from MacDonald Hall before we sat down to refresh our tired limbs. It was a sweet spot, sheltered by a grove of elms from the east and a bed of nettles from the west. Before us ran a babbling brook, and behind us the turnpike road which was to prove so significant in the perils which would continue to distress us.

Chapter Fourteen

I must now warn those who peruse these pages to prepare themselves, for the most pathetic, the most alarming, the most heart-wrenching part of my tale is almost upon you. Read on, therefore, at your peril!

We untied our bonnets and reclined in the shade, supported by our baggage.

'What a lovely scene!' I said at last. 'If only Edward and Augustus were here to share it with us.'

'Oh, Laura!' Sophia cried soulfully. 'What would I not give to learn the fate of my Augustus: to know if he is still in Newgate or if he has already been hanged.'

I placed my arm about her shoulders, attempting to comfort her.

'Shall we return to London, then, dearest?'

'By no means.' She shook her head in a decided negative. 'I shall never be able to conquer my tender sensibility enough to enquire after my beloved. I do not think I can even bear to hear his name again.'

'Never,' I vowed, 'shall I again offend your feelings by mentioning him.'

'Thank you, my dear friend.'

I looked around once more, observing the wild scenery and breaking out rhapsodically, 'Look, Sophia, at the noble grandeur of those elms which shelter us from the eastern zephyr!'

'Yes, the elms.' Sophia gave a sigh of utmost sadness. 'Alas, they remind me of my Augustus. Like them, he was tall and majestic. Do not mention elms, my Laura.'

'No elms,' I murmured, committing this to memory.

In the meantime, I wondered silently what I might say which would not burden Sophia by reminding her of her husband. The sun might remind her of his hair, and the moon of his teeth. The stars would recall the twinkle in his eyes and the water his chamber pot. For several minutes I remained silent, until Sophia's plaintive voice prodded me to attempt further conversation.

'Why do you not speak, Laura?' she asked, in some concern. 'This silence leaves me to my own thoughts, which always return to my Augustus.'

'What a beautiful sky!' I declared, which was the first thing that occurred to me. 'Just look how the azure is varied by those delicate streaks of white cloud.'

Sophia glanced up at the sky in question for a moment, then looked down as tears began to stream from her eyes.

'Oh, Laura,' she wailed, 'do not distress me by calling my attention to an object which so cruelly reminds me of Augustus's blue satin waistcoat with white stripes.'

'Forgive me, Sophia.'

'With pleasure, Laura.'

Her tears gradually ceased, but the silence continued for some minutes. In truth, I had exhausted my store of innocuous comments and knew not what else to say.

Happily, the uncomfortable silence was broken in a most unexpected manner. A low, rumbling noise in the distance had been growing ever nearer, and suddenly there was the sound of horses braying wildly in fear, followed by a terrific crash and the groans of men in severe distress.

Turning our heads, Sophia and I at once spied an overturned phaeton upon the road only a few hundred yards away from us. We surveyed the wreckage with considerable interest as we sat there in mute contemplation for several seconds.

'What a fortunate occurrence,' I remarked at last to my companion. 'Now your mind must be diverted from more melancholy thoughts.'

'Yes indeed,' she agreed. 'I am now so engrossed in the scene before me that I can hardly think of anything else.'

At this, we both stood up, craning our necks in order to obtain a better view of the calamity.

'To think,' I wondered aloud, 'that but a few moments ago these unlucky travellers were elevated so high, but now are laid low and sprawling in the dust.'

By now the horses had managed to break free of the wreckage and were running off, leaving the stricken passengers to their fate.

'That phaeton,' Sophia said, pointing to the carnage, 'and the life of Cardinal Wolsey, provide us ample reflection on the uncertain enjoyments of this world, do they not?'

'It cannot be denied.'

Sophia placed one delicate finger against her chin, considering what to do next. It was a philosophical and ethical conundrum, to be sure.

'Should we perhaps go and see whether we can provide aid to those so afflicted?'

'That might relieve the tedium of our day,' I said.

We strolled towards the wreckage, picking our way slowly and carefully through the tall grass, where thorns encroached and would have torn our delicate skirts had we not been so mindful of them. So we crossed the small field and arrived at the road.

As we drew nearer, we could plainly perceive the prostrate figures of two well-dressed gentlemen. Only a few feet from these poor victims of cruel misfortune, we stopped dead in our tracks. Both of us had perceived something so unexpected and so horrifying as to deprive us of breath and mobility at once: one of the men was plainly attired in a blue-and-white striped waistcoat exactly like the one so lately mentioned by Sophia.

'Oh, Heavens!' she shrieked. 'It is Augustus!'

'And Edward!' I added, my voice little more than a croak.

Sophia reached them first and bent quickly over her husband.

'Gone!' she wailed like a banshee. 'Like the bubble on

the fountain, he is gone, and forever.'

She immediately collapsed in a heap upon the ground while I bent over Edward, who gave a muffled moan and moved ever so slightly.

'He lives!' I cried exultantly.

'Augustus lives?' Sophia gasped, reviving momentarily and raising her head an inch or two from the earth.

'No, no,' I corrected her. 'Edward lives. Augustus is dead.'

Sophia resumed her faint, while I leaned closer to speak to Edward, whose feeble voice was barely audible.

'Laura,' he whispered, 'I fear I have been overturned.'

'I fear you have.' I was eager to reassure him. 'But tell me, I beseech you, what has befallen you since that unhappy day when Augustus was incarcerated and we were cruelly separated?'

'What?'

'What trials have you endured? What persecutions have you suffered?'

He opened his mouth to speak, and I grabbed him by the broad lapels of his fashionable coat, raising his whole body in the intensity of my emotions.

'I . . . I. . . .'

'Speak to me, my Edward!' I demanded. 'Tell me what has happened. Speak, Edward. Speak!'

'I will,' he said, his voice trailing off pitifully.

The words had scarcely been uttered when his eyes rolled up into his head, he fell back like a sack of potatoes, and exhaled his last, halting breath.

What is a young lady to do when her husband drops

dead before he can regale her with his heroic exploits? For me, there was no question what my proper conduct should be. Since this was Scotland, after all, it seemed only right that I should emulate the fabled *Bride of Lammermoor.* Standing up, swaying and moaning, I pulled my long, dark hair into wild disarray.

'Do not talk to me of phaetons!' I shouted at the empty air. 'Give me a violin. I'll play for him and soothe him in his solitude.'

At these words, Sophia revived once more.

'You will play for Augustus?' she pleaded.

'No, for Edward,' I snapped. 'Augustus is still dead, you fool.'

'So is Edward,' she reminded me, somewhat pettishly, I thought.

'Do not interrupt me now,' I said, twirling and dancing through the grass. 'I'm raving mad.'

'Very well, then.' She fainted again, leaving me to enjoy my lunacy in private.

'Beware,' I intoned, glancing this way and that, 'ye gentle nymphs, of Cupid's thunderbolts. Avoid the piercing shafts of Jupiter and the Ides of March.'

I continued in this manner for several hours, until finally night descended. I was quite covered in dirt and scratched with gravel, for I had on several occasions tripped over Sophia's prostrate body.

'Look at that grove of firs!' I soliloquized, my voice at last growing hoarse from my constant vocal exertions. 'I see a leg of mutton! They told me Edward was not dead, but they deceived me. They mistook him for a cucumber!'

'A cucumber sandwich?' Sophia asked, reviving yet again and sitting up. She looked around in bewilderment.

'There's no cucumber sandwich,' I hastened to inform her. 'Where on earth would we find a loaf of bread at this hour?'

'My dear Laura,' she announced, 'night is upon us, the dew is falling fast, and I am weak from hunger.'

'What,' I demanded, 'does any of this matter to a poor, mad widow like me?'

'It matters to a poor, fainting widow like your dear Sophia.'

Tiring of my rant at last, I knelt beside my friend, eager to assist her.

'Forgive me, dearest,' I said, recovering my wits. 'But where can we procure a good, hot meal and shelter from the cold?'

Sophia pointed westward. 'What about that cottage over there?'

I turned, my gaze following her finger to where I soon perceived a large white cottage, perhaps a quarter of a mile away, plainly visible in an unusually bright shaft of silvery moonlight.

'I hadn't noticed that before,' I said in some surprise.

'Neither had I,' Sophia admitted. 'But there it is, as plain as day.'

'Or rather plainer.'

'Perhaps there we shall find some kind soul to take us in for the night.'

I reached down to help Sophia up, suddenly realizing that her gown was quite soaked through with the dew. I was not half as wet as I had been moving about all evening while she'd lain prone upon the ground.

Picking up our cases once more, we made our way slowly towards the cottage, leaving behind the wrecked vehicle and the corpses of our husbands—which we trusted some local official would soon remove and have suitably interred, from motives either sanitary or philanthropic.

It took us more than a few minutes to reach the humble dwelling, for Sophia was much weaker than I, and her faltering steps and constant leaning upon me impeded our progress considerably. At length, however, we arrived at the front door and knocked loudly for admittance.

Chapter Fifteen

The door was at last opened by a stout young country girl named Bridget. The cottage, it seemed, belonged to her grandmother, who was eager to offer us her hospitality. Bridget, I am sorry to say, eyed us with distinct mistrust and was not nearly so accommodating.

Nevertheless, we were given one small room with two narrow beds between us which we gladly accepted. I longed for a rest, for my operatic performance had greatly fatigued me. However, I got precious little sleep, for Sophia's heavy breathing and a hacking cough she had unaccountably developed kept me awake for several hours together. I refrained from remarking upon her incessant noise, however, and stoically endured her thoughtless behaviour.

Sophia never left her bed the next day. That evening, as I sat before a roaring fire with a woollen blanket about my shoulders, Bridget approached me and crudely opened a conversation in spite of my obvious reluctance to speak.

'I fear your friend is very ill,' she said.

'She complains of a violent headache,' I answered, 'aches and pains, flutterings and tremblings all over her.'

'You really should not have been out so late yesterday evening. You should have brought her here before the night came on.'

'My senses were not quite right at the time,' I said defensively, resenting her scolding tone.

'Are you certain that they are recovered now?'

'Of course. Why do you ask?'

She looked me up and down, as if I were a hat in a milliner's shop which she doubted whether she considered worth purchasing.

'You do not seem quite normal to me,' she answered bluntly. 'And my grandmother thinks that your friend has little strength to fight this putrid fever she has developed.'

'Sophia was ever a delicate creature,' I concurred, 'with the most exquisite sensibility.'

'Yes, she looks like someone whose nerves are disordered.'

'It is no such thing!' I cried at once, taking umbrage at the unfeeling way in which she continued to refer to Sophia and myself. 'My friend's feelings are excessively tender and her mind quite exalted.'

Bridget fixed me with her basilisk stare, but only remarked, 'Just as I said.'

I could endure no more of her insolence. Flinging off the blanket and quickly making my way toward the door, I pouted prettily and said, 'I will go to her now.'

'God knows what good you'll do,' Bridget answered sourly.

The bedchamber was neat and tidy, but sparsely furnished. The one small window was closed and the curtains drawn. A single candle on a small stand beside the bed illuminated the sufferer upon it, leaving the rest of the scene in shadow.

Sophia lay in the centre of the bed, her eyes closed and her arms by her side. Her hair was splayed out upon the pillow, and her brow glistened with sweat. I knelt beside her and took her left hand in mine.

'Is Bridget gone?' she queried, not opening her eyes.

'Yes, dearest.'

'She is hopeless.' Sophia pursed her lips. 'She has neither refined ideas nor delicate feelings.'

'She is nothing more than forebearing, civil and obliging.'

'Contemptible!' she agreed. 'But one cannot expect more from someone with a name like *Bridget Jones*.'

Suddenly the enormity of the situation overcame me, and I broke down into a fit of strenuous sobbing, taking up the edge of the sheet and burying my face in it.

'My dearest Sophia,' I cried, 'do not leave me! Do not leave me alone.'

'I fear I must, dear Laura. The angels beckon.'

I raised my head, my eyes wide with terror.

'From which direction?' I asked. 'Above or below?'

Sophia attempted to raise herself up on one elbow, but fell back again at once, too weak to support herself.

'You must be strong.' Her eyelids fluttered. 'My disorder has turned to a galloping consumption that will carry me quite away.'

'Do you really think so?'

'I do indeed.'

'At least,' I said consolingly, 'my attentions to you have ever been above reproach.'

'Yes.'

'I have bathed your sweet face with my tears more than once.'

'You have.'

'I have pressed your hands continually in mine.'

'I have the bruises to prove it.'

She lifted one arm limply, extending it to me. I caught it at once in a crushing grip and she winced slightly.

'Ah!' I moaned softly. 'My poor, dear Sophia.'

'I die a martyr to my grief for the loss of Augustus. One fatal swoon has cost me my life.'

'So it has.'

A strange light seemed to illumine her delicate features, like a Florentine Madonna in a Renaissance painting.

'Hear me, Laura,' she whispered with intensity.

'Yes, dear.'

'Beware of swoons and fainting fits. Though at the time they may seem refreshing, if they are indulged in too frequently and in unseasonable weather, they can be ruinous to one's constitution.'

'True,' I said. 'Alas, too true.'

'A frenzy fit,' she continued, though her voice began to waver, 'is not nearly as pernicious. It is an exercise to the body and ultimately conducive to good health.'

'You are right, as ever, my dear friend.'

She opened her mouth to speak again, but for a moment had not strength enough for words. Her breathing was alarmingly laboured and her voice so weak that I was forced to place my ear almost against her lips to hear her.

'Run mad as often as you like, Laura,' she murmured, 'but do not faint.'

Then, in an instant, her eyes closed for the last time and her arm fell limply from the side of the bed.

'I will ever endeavour,' I vowed fervently, 'to follow your dying wishes, my Sophia.'

At this juncture I felt it appropriate to erupt into a flood of tears and to admit a short, keening wail. As I did so, however, I became aware that I was no longer alone. Bridget had silently entered the chamber and stood just behind me and to my left, looking down at the lifeless form upon the bed.

'Is she gone?' she asked gently.

'Never to return.'

I stood and turned away from Bridget, moving towards the door.

'We must make arrangements for her burial,' the girl said, stopping me in my tracks.

'I will leave that to you,' I said. 'I am too distressed to think of such things.'

Bridget was clearly surprised and apparently not much pleased by this.

'Leave it to me?' she demanded, scowling. 'She was your friend, not mine.'

'But I am quite unequal to such a task,' I protested. 'My sensibility is far too . . . too. . . .'

'Exalted?' she suggested drily.

'Exactly so.' I was pleased at her quick comprehension, which I really had not expected.

'We will discuss this again in the morning.'

With this ominous sentence, she drew the sheet up over Sophia's face while I slipped out of the room as fast as I could.

It was clear to me that the arrangements for Sophia's interment would be very irritating and time-consuming, not to mention expensive. I had neither the inclination nor the funds for such an undertaking. Therefore, I thought it expedient to quit the cottage before Bridget and her grandmother should attempt to coerce me into exertions so unpleasant and unwelcome to me.

Chapter Sixteen

Sometime after midnight, when I judged the two women to be asleep, I packed my small valise and climbed out through the bedroom window. The valise went out first, and I landed on top of it shortly after.

Making my way back to the road, I was thankful to see that someone had indeed removed the wrecked carriage and the remains of our husbands. Nevertheless, I could hardly stay to dwell upon such matters. I walked briskly for almost a mile, panting heavily from the unaccustomed exercise, the valise growing ever heavier as I advanced.

Suddenly I heard behind me the unmistakable sound of a coach-and-four approaching upon the road. In less than a minute it appeared, and I began to wave my arms vigorously to attract the driver's attention. It was, in fact, a stagecoach; it drew to a halt a yard or two ahead of me.

'Please,' I shouted up at the driver, 'tell me, where is this stage going?'

'To Edinburgh, miss,' he replied promptly, doffing his hat.

'And have you any room for a poor widow abandoned and in deep distress?'

'I do indeed, ma'am.'

'Thank you kindly, coachman.'

I handed my small bag up to him, then opened the carriage door and stepped inside, closing the door behind me as we pulled away.

The interior of the coach was far too dark for me to do more than make out that it was almost full. Everyone appeared to be fast asleep. Even so, I managed to squeeze into the nearest corner and hunched up between the window and the warm body of the stranger beside me.

All was silent, except for the loud and extremely uncouth snores emanating from one of the passengers. I sniffed loudly in disgust, but nobody roused themselves, and I soon closed my eyes from sheer fatigue and joined the contented slumberers.

The morning sunlight slanting across my eyes through

the window presently roused me and I looked around to see that my companions had likewise begun to stir. Imagine my surprise when I immediately recognized three who were well-known to me. First I observed Sir Sidney, the father of my late husband; his daughter, the unsympathetic Augusta; and, of all people, my old friend from the Vale of Uske, my dearest Isabel.

I had been but half awake at first, yawning and stretching in an attempt to clear my sleep-addled senses. Now, though, I was shocked into full alertness.

'Great God!' I cried, stupefied. 'Am I dreaming?'

'It seems to me more in the nature of a nightmare,' Augusta commented.

It may appear quite improbable—even impossible—that I should have happened on a conveyance filled with so many of my former acquaintance, all of whom had featured so prominently in my past melodrama. But stranger things have been known to occur. A medieval nun was said to have levitated on several occasions; Jonah once swallowed a whale; and only a few years ago some fishermen near Portugal hauled a mermaid up in their net—though she managed to escape, I'm told.

But if three acquaintances should seem difficult to credit, eight must be nothing short of miraculous. Still, that is precisely how many of my old acquaintance were travelling with me.

The other five consisted of Edward's Aunt Philippa and her husband, who were driving the coach. I was quite astonished by this eccentricity, but it turned out the explanation was perfectly reasonable. Apparently, Philippa's husband had already spent all her fortune, and they had nothing left to them but their old coach, which they converted into a stage. This allowed him to return to his former occupation, which was all he had ever known before their marriage. As to why they were in Scotland when Philippa's home had been in Middlesex, it was simply a question of pride: they could not very well remain in their old home as stagecoach drivers. They would have been a complete laughing stock to their friends and neighbours.

I had scarcely recovered from the shock of this revelation when I realized that the lady seated beside Edward's sister was none other than the infamous Lady Dorothea—the very same woman whom my Edward was to have married, had he heeded his father's advice. She was, after all, a bosom friend of Augusta's.

Finally—and most fantastic of all, perhaps—I soon discovered that the two gentlemen seated in the basket at the rear of the carriage were none other than Philander and Gustavus!

When Lady Dorothea realized the connection between me and all the others, she could not refrain from exclaiming, 'This is really too much!'

'Yes,' I agreed, 'the coach is a little overcrowded, but not so uncomfortable as one might expect.'

'No,' she corrected me with a snap, 'I mean . . . Oh, never mind!'

I was rather annoyed by her attitude, but turned my attention once more to those two dear boys, Gustavus and Philander. I know that they had been in my black books since robbing Sophia and me of our inheritance. But once I met them again, and realized afresh how very good-looking and charming they both were, what could I do but forgive them for their harmless little peccadilloes? Indeed, we soon found ourselves getting along quite famously when we stopped for a rest at the nearest inn.

It was then, however, that Sir Sidney, Augusta and Lady Dorothea all chose to confront me. The look on the faces of the first two was one of heartless malice. Only my dear Isabel—friend of my childhood—eyed me with bewilderment and curiosity rather than distaste. Naturally, it was into her arms that I presently flung myself.

'Oh! My Isabel,' I cried, clinging desperately to her, 'receive once more to your bosom the unfortunate Laura!'

'Really, Laura.' Isabel's response was not at all what I had expected. She seemed more annoyed than sympathetic. 'There is no need for such an emotional display,' she added coldly. 'Besides, my bosom is not very large, and can receive only so much.'

I pulled away from her a few inches, but continued to address her, ignoring the others.

'But you little know, dear friend, what I have endured.' I wiped a tear from the corner of my eye. 'I am now both an orphan and a widow. . . .'

A simultaneous gasp from Sir Sidney and his daughter expressed their shock, for they had hitherto been quite unaware of the death of their son and brother respectively.

'What has become of my poor brother?' Augusta demanded. 'Is he truly dead?'

'Yes,' I said, turning to face her with a disdain even haughtier than her own. 'Now, cold and insensible nymph, you may glory in being the sole heiress of your father's vast fortune.'

This disclosure produced what I can only describe as the most tepid effect on those whose hearts should have been shattered into a million little pieces. Sir Sidney bit his lips and turned pale, while Augusta's eyes welled with tears. Neither wailed nor tore their clothes and hair. I considered it quite a shabby way to mourn the dearly departed.

Isabel remained perfectly calm—which I could forgive her since she had never known my Edward. It was she who put the next question to me.

'Pray tell us what happened to your husband, Laura.'

I took a deep breath, and then recounted to them all that I have already written in this little book: how we sought shelter with Augustus and Sophia, the arrest of the former and the disappearance of Edward in search of him. I told how Sophia and I had searched the desolate streets of London, how we met our grandfather at a strange inn (only leaving out the behaviour of Gustavus and Philander, which I thought the assembled company might not be as generous about as I was). I narrated how we journeyed into Scotland and assisted MacDonald's daughter; and finally, my voice quite in shreds, I told of the death of Edward, Augustus and Sophia.

'And that, to put it briefly,' I concluded, 'is how you came to find me on the road to Edinburgh, with nothing in my pockets, save a few shillings I purl . . . I received from Bridget's old grandmother.'

'But you seem to have no remorse at all for your

behaviour, Laura,' Isabel said accusingly.

I was quite bewildered by her attitude. I had expected her praise, not her censure.

'For what should I feel remorse?' I enquired proudly.

'But for you,' Augusta interjected, 'my brother might be alive today!'

'In all fairness, Augusta,' Lady Dorothea put in quite unexpectedly, 'Edward's own stupidity had as much to do with his demise as anything this woman has done.'

'I have always behaved in a manner which I believe reflected honour upon my feelings and refinement,' I proclaimed, still exasperated by the way they appeared to view my predicament.

I plainly saw Augusta roll her eyes and shake her head in a gesture of the utmost contempt. Isabel, at least, was not so crude.

'I'm sure you imagine so,' she said, making at least some attempt to understand me. 'And imagination, I suppose, is everything these days.'

'I can bear no more of your baseless accusations!' I cried, leaping to my feet and almost ready to flee once more. In this, however, I was forestalled by Sir Sidney himself.

'Well, madam,' he said, taking a deep breath and addressing me with exquisite formality, if not with joy, 'with all your manifest faults, you are still the widow of my only son. I will see that you are provided with a suitable establishment at a considerable distance from myself—and necessary living expenses, of course.'

'So I should hope!' I faced him proudly. 'Though it would have been more to the credit of your sensibility if you agreed to provide for me because I am the refined and amiable Laura.'

'That,' his tart-tongued daughter said, 'is a matter of opinion on which some of us will beg leave to disagree.'

'However that may be,' Sir Sidney continued, 'you may yet be carrying within you my unborn grandchild. As such, it behoves me to care for you to the best of my ability.'

'That contingency is most unlikely,' Lady Dorothea interjected. 'Edward seems to have been more intimate with Augustus than with Laura.'

Sir Sidney frowned, but only said, 'Nevertheless, I will do my duty by her.'

So it was settled, and I was rewarded in some measure for my sorrows and misfortunes.

Chapter Seventeen

Thus ended the adventures of my youth. Both love and friendship were forever lost to me, for I never found another husband to compare with Edward, though I have twice since tried the married state with much the same result. Nor has there ever appeared in my circle a friend like the lovely Sophia.

With the money provided by Sir Sidney, I retired to this remote spot, forever to lament the death of my mother, father, husband and friends. Of course, mourning, as everyone must be aware, can be quite an exhausting business. I am constrained to renew my strength with the occasional party, ball, or theatrical entertainment.

As for the others, all remain much the same to this day, with the exception of poor Philippa, who has long since gone to her reward; her husband still drives the stage to Edinburgh, however. Sir Sidney married Lady Dorothea, to the mutual advantage of both their fortunes; and Augusta so far debased herself as to wed a Frenchman. Philander and Gustavus went on the stage, performing in panto-mimes and other entertainments, under the names of Lewis and Quick. I often attend their performances when I am in London for the season. Isabel returned to Ireland for a time, then established herself in Bath as one of the pillars of Polite Society.

As for me, nothing can ever offer consolation for all I have endured, nor erase the memories which time merely burnishes to an ever-glistening lustre. The loss of my One True Love, Edward, is a tragedy which has blighted my entire life. I therefore conclude with this word of advice to all young ladies of tender sensibilities: preserve yourself from a First Love and you need not fear a Second.

Take heed, dear reader, from my fate. And so, adieu.

PART THREE

(Marianne's Conclusion)

The preceding narrative is not, in fact, a complete record of the life and exploits of Laura. Nor does it do justice to at least one of the other unfortunates who figures in her story. The recounting of Laura's last days is an arduous task that has been left to my own feeble pen, but it was one that I could not, in all good conscience, neglect.

I visited Laura's home on three occasions over the course of a fortnight in order to read aloud her effusive prose. When at last I had finished, she expressed herself as being intensely gratified by hearing her words given voice, which accolade I accorded all the respect of which I felt it to be worthy.

'I'm afraid,' I told her then, rising from my seat, 'that I must be going. The evening is far advanced, and my mother expects me for supper.'

'But stay,' she abjured me mysteriously. 'Before you go, allow me to reveal to you the heart of my humble house.'

'If you insist.'

She led me down a narrow hallway to a small ante-room

festooned almost entirely in black draperies. As we passed through the doorway, directly facing us was a large demi-lune table above which hung two portraits. One was of a somewhat gloomy-looking young man and the other a desiccated blonde. The table was covered with about a dozen votive candles, looking more like an overdressed church altar. They provided the only light, making the rest of the room appear like a small cave or grotto.

Coming up behind her, I could see that each portrait was draped with a swag of black velvet which puddled against the wall at the back of the table.

'Here, Marianne,' she said in hushed tones, 'is the shrine to my lost love, my vanished hopes and dreams.'

'These portraits, I suppose, are those of your husband and your friend?'

'They are.'

She then reached down and picked up two miniatures which lay flat upon the table before the candles. Holding one in each palm, she displayed them for my delectation.

'These are my parents, and here on the table is also a silhouette of Augustus.'

'A fitting tribute,' I said conventionally, 'to those who are gone.'

'It is the least that I can do.'

As she spoke, she turned away to replace the two portraits and I heard her gasp. Puzzled, I looked at the table where her own gaze was fixed, and noticed that one of the candles on it had burnt out.

To my astonishment, she turned back toward me with a face so contorted with rage that it scarcely seemed human.

'Gladys!' she screeched at the top of her lungs. 'Gladys, come here this instant!'

'What is the matter, ma'am?' I enquired, quite concerned at the purple hue of her countenance.

She ignored me completely, moving swiftly to the door. As she reached it, a maid (whom I correctly assumed to be the missing Gladys) passed through into the room, a look of terror on her face. She was a thin, timid-looking girl, who was clasping her hands together and looking everywhere but at the face of her mistress.

'Gladys,' Laura almost growled at her like a half-crazed feline, 'did I not tell you never—under any circumstances—to let one of these candles burn out?'

'Yes madam.' Gladys shook like a tower in the Lisbon earthquake.

I watched in fascinated disgust as Laura proceeded to grab the maid's left ear and use it to drag her over to her shrine, where she pointed an accusing finger at the extinguished candle.

'Look at that!' she demanded. 'Look at it, you miserable creature!'

Gladys, her head twisted sideways as she squirmed in obvious pain, managed to stammer out, 'Yes, ma'am.'

'Does that look as if it is still lit?' She paused, more for effect, I thought, than in expectation of an answer. 'Well, does it?'

'No, ma'am. I'm ever so sorry, ma'am.'

Laura twisted the ear yet harder, and Gladys buckled at the knees.

'Have you no sensibility, girl?' Laura asked.

'Can't afford it, ma'am,' Gladys objected.

'Have you no compassion?' her tormentor continued. 'No empathy?'

'Don't know what that is.'

At this point, I could no longer refrain from interrupting this absurd mixture of farce and sadism.

'Really, Mrs Lindsay,' I said with some asperity, 'I do not know what else you can expect from the poor child. It is no great matter, after all.'

The veins in her neck stood out so prominently that I would not have been surprised had her head shot up through the ceiling like a rocket.

'No great matter!' she echoed, her whole body clenched and taut. 'After having read my story, I do not know how you can say something so heartless.'

'No real harm has been done,' I insisted, wearied by her self-aggrandizing romanticism.

'This space is sacred, my dear Marianne.' She held herself perfectly erect and confronted me like an ancient Christian martyr facing the lions in the arena. 'What this girl has done is a desecration, I tell you: a sheer desecration.'

'I hardly think that either Sophia or Edward will offer any objection.'

She released Gladys, who promptly put a hand up to her poor ear—which was now an angry red after such strenuous abuse.

'That you can treat this as a jest,' Laura said, 'is a testimony to your insensibility. I see that you are unworthy of the confidence I have placed in you. Once more I am betrayed!'

'Can I go now, ma'am?' Gladys enquired, preventing me from answering this ringing philippic.

'Yes,' her mistress agreed, not bothering to look at her, but continuing to stare at her much-vaunted shrine. 'Go and see that the candle is replaced. When I return, all of them had best be burning, or you will feel my cane across your back, you ungrateful wretch.'

Gladys passed by me on her way out the door, but glanced back at Mrs Lindsay with such a look of hatred and anger on her face that I was quite startled. Her lips compressed in a tight line for a moment before she uttered a strange reply which I have never forgotten: 'Don't worry, ma'am. *Everything* will be burning, all right!'

A few moments later, I was at the front door, making my exit. Laura had not bothered to accompany me, as she was plainly offended by my previous comments. I was not sorry to be so slighted, however, having had quite enough of her by this time, and it was with a feeling of relief that I heard the door close behind me as I made my way down the front steps to the waiting carriage.

Nothing could have prepared me for the news which reached our house the next morning. One of our maids rushed in as Mama and I were at breakfast. She could scarcely get the words out in her frantic eagerness.

'Have you heard, ma'am?' she cried, addressing my mother.

'Heard what?' Mama asked, mystified.

'Your friend, Mrs Lindsay, is dead!'

'Indeed!' Mama remarked. 'Some good news, for a change.'

As to what happened to Laura, I have pieced together the following train of events, based on my subsequent interviews with her servants, who were all most obliging in relating what they knew had transpired after my departure that fateful evening.

About quarter of an hour after I had left, the staff became aware of the faint smell of smoke in the house. Before anyone could investigate the source, a piercing scream broke the silence.

'Gladys!' The voice of their mistress penetrated through even the thickest walls, followed by high-pitched wails of anguish. Everyone rushed to the spot whence the sounds continued to emanate.

Agnes, one of the under-housemaids, arrived at the shrine first, to see the table and the heavy draped fabric all ablaze and the flames licking up the walls behind them.

'Oh, help!' Laura was shouting now. 'Fire! Someone come quickly!'

It was notable, Agnes said, that Laura made no attempt to put out the blaze herself. She merely stood, staring in horrified fascination.

Two other maids rushed in after Agnes. They immediately perceived the urgency of the situation and grabbed whatever they could—aprons, petticoats, their mistress's shawl—and proceeded to beat out the leaping flames before they could spread to the rest of the house. All the while, Laura stood mutely while everyone whirled about her in their frantic fight with the fire.

Eventually the blaze was extinguished, but the shrine

had been irreparably damaged. It was clearly too much for the near-catatonic Laura.

'Are you quite well, ma'am?' Agnes asked, but Laura was apparently incapable of speech by this time, and merely emitted something like a distressed tweet.

'She's had a bad shock,' one of the other maids commented.

As the maid finished speaking, the portrait of Edward, which was still intact, though badly singed, fell from the wall and landed on the floor with a loud crash. This broke the spell which had held Laura silent.

'Oh, my Edward!' she wailed. Then, putting her hand to her head, she began to sway alarmingly, while the servants clustered around, trying to hold her up.

'She's goin' to swoon!' one of them cried.

'You mean faint?' Agnes asked.

'That's right.'

'She never faints,' Agnes asserted. 'It's a rule.'

'Well, she's going to break it now!'

Laura slumped to the floor, unconscious.

'There she goes,' another maid said.

They knelt down beside her, holding her head and fanning her. One fetched a bottle of *sal ammonia*, which remedy proved to be useless.

'Get Gladys to fetch the doctor!' Agnes ordered, taking charge of the situation.

'Nobody can't find Gladys,' said the youngest maid. 'She's run off.'

'I wish I'd had the wits to do the same!'

'I never thought I'd see the day!' Agnes shook her head

in wonder. 'I'll wager it's the end of her.'

This dire prophecy was quickly proved to be accurate. The doctor arrived within another half-hour, but his countenance was grim after examining the patient. She had sustained a severe shock, which proved to be too much for her delicate constitution. Before the following morning, Laura Lindsay was no more.

Unfortunately, even in death, she continued to be a plague upon those who knew her. Not only was I entrusted with her precious manuscript, but my mother also was constrained to bear some of the burden surrounding her demise. Laura's father-in-law, Sir Sidney, was desirous of erecting a suitable monument to the widow of his beloved son, but could think of no words (or none which might reasonably be chiselled into a headstone for public perusal) to describe so peculiar a person. In the end, he appealed to my mother, as Laura's oldest friend, to supply something appropriate. This was a nearly impossible task which sorely vexed us both.

Barely a fortnight after Laura's demise, Mama and I sat in the salon, discussing the question.

'A most unfortunate and unexpected accident, to be sure,' I noted. 'One must be grateful that the entire house did not burn to the ground.'

Mama took a sip of tea.

'I always thought that Laura would live forever,' she said, 'if only to spite Sir Sidney.'

'He has placed quite a burden upon your shoulders.'

'Yes.' She sighed. 'That pernicious woman gives me no peace, even from beyond the grave.'

'Still, in all fairness, you are the most fitting person to compose an epitaph for her.'

'But what can one say about a woman who dies—especially a woman like Laura?'

I set my own cup back into its saucer, considering the matter.

'One must say something—even if it is less than honest.'

'Indeed.'

'It is customary to mention the virtues of the departed.'

'If only one could think of any!'

'Well,' I said, after some more minutes of thought, 'there are those who consider loving oneself to be a virtue.'

'In that case,' Mama assured me, 'Laura was the most virtuous woman who ever lived!'

'Her journal was the most incredible document I have ever read,' I remarked. 'I could scarcely credit it.'

'Unfortunately, most of it was quite true.'

'I wonder whatever became of poor Janetta?'

My mother adjusted a pearl necklace she wore, and gave a sincere sigh.

'She perished giving birth to her fifth child.'

'She had five children by Captain M'Kenrie?' I asked, astonished.

'She did.' Mama nodded assent. 'By the time the fifth was born, of course, M'Kenrie had abandoned her. The children are being brought up by their grandfather at MacDonald Hall.'

'How sad.' I had hoped that fate would be kinder to the young Scottish lass.

'At least,' Mama reasoned, 'her eldest son, Ronald, will

inherit her father's estate and become the leader of Clan MacDonald.'

'Small consolation for a ruined life,' I noted.

'But what of you, my dear?' Mama leaned forward and held my hand in hers. 'Have you made a decision regarding your betrothal to Tom?'

I nodded. 'I am going to marry him.'

'You seem much more confident in your assertion.' She raised a provocative eyebrow. 'But Tom is not as wealthy as John Isherwood, nor so handsome nor dashing as that rake, Sir Charles.'

'True.' I smiled saucily. 'But he is good and kind. I fancy that I would not find it irksome to spend the rest of my life in his company.'

'He is no hero, like the noble Augustus and Edward.' She could not resist a jibe at the late Mrs Lindsay's expense.

'And I am neither Laura nor Sophia.'

'Your sensibilities are not so exquisite, perhaps?'

'I fear that I am hampered by having far too much sense.'

She sighed with complete satisfaction.

'That,' she said, 'is a blemish which I am happy to overlook.'

'Now I can look forward to my wedding without trepidation.'

'I am glad for your sake, Marianne. But I am no nearer to solving my own problem.'

I pursed my lips, returning my attention to the task of finding something to say about the recently departed.

'One could say, at least,' I suggested, 'that Laura was true to herself, as Shakespeare might put it.'

My mother gave a not very genteel snort of pure derision.

'So,' she said, 'was Napoleon. So, indeed, was Satan! Every lover follows their own heart, as does every pudding-head and every scoundrel.'

I groaned, feeling that we had failed yet again.

'If only,' I muttered my thoughts aloud, 'she had not swooned that evening.'

To my surprise, Mama brightened at once. She looked as if a burden had truly been lifted from her shoulders.

'My darling child,' she said, embracing me in her sudden and apparently unalloyed joy, 'you have hit upon the very thing. I know now precisely what must be said!'

She went to her desk and pulled out a sheet of fresh white paper, taking quill in hand and beginning to write.

'What is it?' I asked, burning with curiosity.

'Words,' she answered, 'which I think Sir Sidney will find more than acceptable.'

It was several months before the marble statue—depicting a veiled lady swooning in a chair—was placed upon Laura's grave in the nearby churchyard. Mama and I made a kind of pilgrimage there, to see for ourselves how her words looked when carved in stone.

As we stood before the unusual memorial, I read aloud the inscription etched before us:

'"Here lies Laura Lindsay,
a most remarkable woman.
She was the victim of
one fatal mistake:

she fainted when she
should have run mad."'

As we stood there, silently observing Laura's final resting place, a stray mongrel ran up to the imposing marble monument, lifted his leg and proceeded to empty his bladder over the base.

'Well,' said Mama, 'I thought that my epitaph was the most fitting that could be found for Laura. I fear, however, that I have been outdone by a dog!'

THE END

AFTERWORD:
REWRITING JANE AUSTEN

Jane Austen's writings have spawned a cottage industry of prequels, sequels and re-inventions based on her various novels. Almost every character in *Pride and Prejudice*, for example, has been cast as the hero or heroine (or, occasionally, anti-heroine) of some new novel. There have been murders at Pemberley, adulterous affairs, and enough transatlantic voyages to make even Captain Wentworth seasick. Any day now I expect to see a review of a book detailing the exploits of the jilted heiress, Miss King, or a fantasy based on the pigs who occasionally got into the Collins' garden. After all, we have already been assaulted by zombies and sea monsters, so we should hardly be surprised to find Martians landing at Netherfield Hall, for instance.

What Jane Austen would have thought of all of this is a moot point. I suspect she would have been highly amused, as she was by the popular novels of her own day.

My own foray into this field is somewhat different. I felt there was little I could add to Jane's six mature novels, but her juvenilia was another matter. I always had a fondness for *Love and Freindship*, but considered that a little more flesh might well be added to what are essentially only the bare bones of a story. Rather than 'lopping and cropping', I have 'added and padded', freely employing occasional episodes or quotes from other Austen juvenilia, inventing additional dialogue (the main part of my revision), giving a little more substance to Marianne's character, and creating a totally new ending.

My desire was to remain true to the somewhat subversive tone, and keep as much of the original material as possible, while fleshing it out and making it a bit more relevant for the contemporary reader. How well I've succeeded is not for me to judge.

It is surely one of the great literary ironies that Jane Austen is now almost universally categorized as a writer of romantic fiction. That is not how her contemporaries and immediate successors viewed her, however.

Sir Walter Scott, who was one of the first to recognize her peculiar genius, was moved (after reading *Emma*) to waste a lengthy paragraph in defence of Cupid. Charlotte Bronte's response to the same novel was one of supreme contempt. Even Anthony Trollope proclaimed, 'Miss Austen has no romance: none at all.'

Jane Austen was, in fact, the arch-enemy of romance. This may seem a curious statement, considering that all of her books revolve around young women searching for the 'perfect husband'. It must be remembered, however, that their search was intensely practical, involving head as well as heart. Jane may have had little use for those who married 'without affection', as she warned her niece, Fanny, but she was equally contemptuous of those who chose their life partner purely on the basis of emotions which were often as misleading as they were ephemeral.

If one wants to see how she felt about the romantic novels of her time, one only has to dip into her juvenilia—of which *Love and Freindship* is probably the best-known and most accessible example.

In the real world, marriage provided a woman with security and stability, cementing her social status. It was, therefore, immensely important to choose wisely, because the stakes were outrageously high. Once married, a woman was more or less subject to her husband. Emotional fulfilment was often not even a consideration.

On the other hand, Jane Austen depicts a variety of marriage relationships throughout her work. Mr Bennet, for instance, has been hounded into retreat by his wife's incessant nagging and whining. Lady Bertram, however, is completely dependent upon her husband and has declined into near-inertia. It is clear that women like Lady Catherine de Bourgh and Aunt Norris were never doormats, but more likely domestic tyrants; while some, like Mrs Collins, firmly but tactfully manipulate their befuddled husbands with a fatalistic resignation to their lot.

There are, moreover, happy marriages in the novels. The Gardiners and the Crofts immediately come to mind, as pretty much equal partnerships where there is mutual respect and forbearance. If Jane does not dwell on these, it is surely because they are not nearly as funny as the dysfunctional relationships which she mined so effectively for her comic purposes.

The marriages and friendships portrayed in *Love and Freindship* are, of course, mere caricatures of those propounded by Rousseau and the romantic novelists. This is satire at its most iconoclastic: outrageous lampoons intended mainly to entertain Jane's relatives with their exaggerated portraits.

No less a writer than G.K. Chesterton provided a preface for the 1922 publication of Austen's juvenile fiction. In it, he pinpoints the 'secret' of her greatness: she was, he says, 'naturally exuberant'. Her ability to control her exuberance is what gives 'an infallible force to her irony' and 'a stunning weight to her understatements'.

In her later work, Jane Austen achieved an even greater control over that exuberance, and her irony became more powerful than ever. Some have lamented that she abandoned the overt and almost unrestrained comedy of her early work. They see her later work as restricted, perhaps even repressed. Subtlety and self-control are not qualities to which modern readers respond positively, it seems. However, they represent precisely her maturity and growth as an artist.

Had she continued in the vein of her teenage years, she would have been at best a 'cult' classic: a writer admired by some but known by few. But she grew up, and her work grew up along with her. Nevertheless, the exuberance Chesterton admired is most attractively displayed in works like *Love and Freindship,* and is the quality I have struggled to capture in my own re-telling of this youthful *jeau d'esprit.*

LOVE
AND
FREINDSHIP

TO MADAME LA COMTESSE DE FEUILLIDE THIS NOVEL IS INSCRIBED BY HER OBLIGED HUMBLE SERVANT

THE AUTHOR.

"Deceived in Freindship and Betrayed in Love."

LETTER the FIRST From ISABEL to LAURA

How often, in answer to my repeated intreaties that you would give my Daughter a regular detail of the Misfortunes and Adventures of your Life, have you said "No, my freind never will I comply with your request till I may be no longer in Danger of again experiencing such dreadful ones."

Surely that time is now at hand. You are this day 55. If a woman may ever be said to be in safety from the determined Perseverance of disagreeable Lovers and the cruel Persecutions of obstinate Fathers, surely it must be at such a time of Life. Isabel

LETTER 2nd LAURA to ISABEL

Altho' I cannot agree with you in supposing that I shall never again be exposed to Misfortunes as unmerited as those I have already experienced, yet to avoid the imputation of Obstinacy or ill-nature, I will gratify the curiosity of your daughter; and may the fortitude with which I have suffered the many afflictions of my past Life, prove to her a useful lesson for the support of those which may befall her in her own. Laura

LETTER 3rd LAURA to MARIANNE

As the Daughter of my most intimate freind I think you entitled to that knowledge of my unhappy story, which your Mother has so often solicited me to give you.

My Father was a native of Ireland and an inhabitant of Wales; my Mother was the natural Daughter of a Scotch Peer by an italian Opera-girl—I was born in Spain and received my Education at a Convent in France.

When I had reached my eighteenth Year I was recalled by my Parents to my paternal roof in Wales. Our mansion was situated in one of the most romantic parts of the Vale of Uske. Tho' my Charms are now considerably softened and somewhat impaired by the Misfortunes I have undergone, I was once beautiful. But lovely as I was the Graces of my Person were the least of my Perfections. Of every accomplishment accustomary to my sex, I was Mistress. When in the Convent, my progress had always exceeded my instructions, my Acquirements had been wonderfull for my age, and I had shortly surpassed my Masters.

In my Mind, every Virtue that could adorn it was centered; it was the Rendez-vous of every good Quality and of every noble sentiment.

A sensibility too tremblingly alive to every affliction of my Freinds, my Acquaintance and particularly to every affliction of my own, was my only fault, if a fault it could be called. Alas! how altered now! Tho' indeed my own Misfortunes do not make less impression on me than they ever did, yet now I never feel for those of an other. My accomplishments too, begin to fade—I can neither sing so well nor Dance so gracefully as I once did—and I have entirely forgot the MINUET DELA COUR. Adeiu. Laura.

LETTER 4th Laura to MARIANNE

Our neighbourhood was small, for it consisted only of your Mother. She may probably have already told you that being left by her Parents in indigent Circumstances she had retired into Wales on eoconomical motives. There it was our freindship first commenced. Isobel was then one and twenty. Tho' pleasing both in her Person and Manners (between ourselves) she never possessed the hundredth part of my Beauty or Accomplishments. Isabel had seen the World. She had passed 2 Years at one of the first Boarding-schools in London; had spent a fortnight in Bath and had supped one night in Southampton.

"Beware my Laura (she would often say) Beware of the insipid Vanities and idle Dissipations of the Metropolis of England; Beware of the unmeaning Luxuries of Bath and of the stinking fish of Southampton."

"Alas! (exclaimed I) how am I to avoid those evils I shall never be exposed to? What probability is there of my ever tasting the Dissipations of London, the Luxuries of Bath, or the stinking Fish of Southampton? I who am doomed to waste my Days of Youth and Beauty in an humble Cottage in the Vale of Uske."

Ah! little did I then think I was ordained so soon to quit that humble Cottage for the Deceitfull Pleasures of the World. Adeiu Laura.

LETTER 5th LAURA to MARIANNE

One Evening in December as my Father, my Mother and myself, were arranged in social converse round our Fireside, we were on a sudden greatly astonished, by hearing a violent knocking on the outward door of our rustic Cot.

My Father started—"What noise is that," (said he.) "It sounds like a loud rapping at the door"—(replied my Mother.) "it does indeed." (cried I.) "I am of your opinion; (said my Father) it certainly does appear to proceed from some uncommon violence exerted against our unoffending door." "Yes (exclaimed I) I cannot help thinking it must be somebody who knocks for admittance."

"That is another point (replied he;) We must not pretend to determine on what motive the person may knock—tho' that someone DOES rap at the door, I am partly convinced."

Here, a 2d tremendous rap interrupted my Father in his speech, and somewhat alarmed my Mother and me.

"Had we better not go and see who it is? (said she) the servants are out." "I think we had." (replied I.) "Certainly, (added my Father) by all means." "Shall we go now?" (said my Mother,) "The sooner the better." (answered he.) "Oh! let no time be lost" (cried I.)

A third more violent Rap than ever again assaulted our ears. "I am certain there is somebody knocking at the Door." (said my Mother.) "I think there must," (replied my Father) "I fancy the servants are returned; (said I) I think I hear Mary going to the Door." "I'm glad of it (cried my Father) for I long to know who it is."

I was right in my conjecture; for Mary instantly entering the Room, informed us that a young Gentleman and his Servant were at the door, who had lossed their way, were very cold and begged leave to warm themselves by our fire.

"Won't you admit them?" (said I.) "You have no objection, my Dear?" (said my Father.) "None in the World." (replied my Mother.)

Mary, without waiting for any further commands immediately left the room and quickly returned introducing the most beauteous and amiable Youth, I had ever beheld. The servant she kept to herself.

My natural sensibility had already been greatly affected by the sufferings of the unfortunate stranger and no sooner did I first behold him, than I felt that on him the happiness or Misery of my future Life must depend. Adeiu Laura.

LETTER 6th LAURA to MARIANNE

The noble Youth informed us that his name was Lindsay—for particular reasons however I shall conceal it under that of Talbot. He told us that he was the son of an English Baronet, that his Mother had been for many years no more and that he had a Sister of the middle size. "My Father (he continued) is a mean and mercenary wretch—it is only to such particular freinds as this Dear Party that I would thus betray his failings. Your Virtues my amiable Polydore (addressing himself to my father) yours Dear Claudia and yours my Charming Laura call on me to repose in you, my confidence." We bowed. "My Father seduced by the false glare of Fortune and the Deluding Pomp of Title, insisted on my giving my hand to Lady Dorothea. No never exclaimed I. Lady Dorothea is lovely and Engaging; I prefer no woman to her; but know Sir, that I scorn to marry her in compliance with your Wishes. No! Never shall it be said that I obliged my Father."

We all admired the noble Manliness of his reply. He continued.

"Sir Edward was surprised; he had perhaps little expected to meet with so spirited an opposition to his will. "Where, Edward in the name of wonder (said he) did you pick up this unmeaning gibberish? You have been studying Novels I suspect." I scorned to answer: it would have been beneath my dignity. I mounted my Horse and followed by my faithful William set forth for my Aunts."

"My Father's house is situated in Bedfordshire, my Aunt's in Middlesex, and tho' I flatter myself with being a tolerable proficient in Geography, I know not how it happened, but I found myself entering this beautifull Vale which I find is in South Wales, when I had expected to have reached my Aunts."

"After having wandered some time on the Banks of the Uske without knowing which way to go, I began to lament my cruel Destiny in the bitterest and most pathetic Manner. It was now perfectly dark, not a single star was there to direct my steps, and I know not what might have befallen me had I not at length discerned thro' the solemn Gloom that surrounded me a distant light, which as I approached it, I discovered to be the chearfull Blaze of your fire. Impelled by the combination of Misfortunes under which I laboured, namely Fear, Cold and Hunger I hesitated not to ask admittance which at length I have gained; and now my Adorable Laura (continued he taking my Hand) when may I hope to receive that reward of all the painfull sufferings I have undergone during the course of my attachment to you, to which I have ever aspired. Oh! when will you reward me with Yourself?"

"This instant, Dear and Amiable Edward." (replied I.). We were immediately united by my Father, who tho' he had never taken orders had been bred to the Church. Adeiu Laura

LETTER 7th LAURA to MARIANNE

We remained but a few days after our Marriage, in the Vale of Uske. After taking an affecting Farewell of my Father, my Mother and my Isabel, I accompanied Edward to his Aunt's in Middlesex. Philippa received us both with every expression of affectionate Love. My arrival was indeed a most agreable surprise to her as she had not only been totally ignorant of my Marriage with her Nephew, but had never even had the slightest idea of there being such a person in the World.

Augusta, the sister of Edward was on a visit to her when we arrived. I found her exactly what her Brother had described her to be—of the middle size. She received me with equal surprise though not with equal Cordiality, as Philippa. There was a disagreable coldness and Forbidding Reserve in her reception of me which was equally distressing and Unexpected. None of that interesting Sensibility or amiable simpathy in her manners and Address to me when we first met which should have distinguished our introduction to each other. Her Language was neither warm, nor affectionate, her expressions of regard were neither animated nor cordial; her arms were not opened to receive me to her Heart, tho' my own were extended to press her to mine.

A short Conversation between Augusta and her Brother, which I accidentally overheard encreased my dislike to her, and convinced me that her Heart was no more formed for the soft ties of Love than for the endearing intercourse of Freindship.

"But do you think that my Father will ever be reconciled to this imprudent connection?" (said Augusta.)

"Augusta (replied the noble Youth) I thought you had a better opinion of me, than to imagine I would so abjectly degrade myself as to consider my Father's Concurrence in any of my affairs, either of Consequence or concern to me. Tell me Augusta with sincerity; did you ever know me consult his inclinations or follow his Advice in the least trifling Particular since the age of fifteen?"

"Edward (replied she) you are surely too diffident in your own praise. Since you were fifteen only! My Dear Brother since you were five years old, I entirely acquit you of ever having willingly contributed to the satisfaction of your Father. But still I am not without apprehensions of your being shortly obliged to degrade yourself in your own eyes by seeking a support for your wife in the Generosity of Sir Edward."

"Never, never Augusta will I so demean myself. (said Edward). Support! What support will Laura want which she can receive from him?"

"Only those very insignificant ones of Victuals and Drink." (answered she.)

"Victuals and Drink! (replied my Husband in a most nobly contemptuous Manner) and dost thou then imagine that there is no other support for an exalted mind (such as is my Laura's) than the mean and indelicate employment of Eating and Drinking?"

"None that I know of, so efficacious." (returned Augusta).

"And did you then never feel the pleasing Pangs of Love, Augusta? (replied my Edward). Does it appear impossible to your vile and corrupted Palate, to exist on Love? Can you not conceive the Luxury of living in every distress that Poverty can inflict, with the object of your tenderest affection?"

"You are too ridiculous (said Augusta) to argue with; perhaps however you may in time be convinced that..."

Here I was prevented from hearing the remainder of her speech, by the appearance of a very Handsome young Woman, who was ushured into the Room at the Door of which I had been listening. On hearing her announced by the Name of "Lady Dorothea," I instantly quitted my Post and followed her into the Parlour, for I well remembered that she was the Lady, proposed as a Wife for my Edward by the Cruel and Unrelenting Baronet.

Altho' Lady Dorothea's visit was nominally to Philippa and Augusta, yet I have some reason to imagine that (acquainted with the Marriage and arrival of Edward) to see me was a principal motive to it.

I soon perceived that tho' Lovely and Elegant in her Person and tho' Easy and Polite in her Address, she was of that inferior order of Beings with regard to Delicate Feeling, tender Sentiments, and refined Sensibility, of which Augusta was one.

She staid but half an hour and neither in the Course of her Visit, confided to me any of her secret thoughts, nor requested me to confide in her, any of Mine. You will easily imagine therefore my Dear Marianne that I could not feel any ardent affection or very sincere Attachment for Lady Dorothea. Adeiu Laura.

LETTER 8th LAURA to MARIANNE, in continuation

Lady Dorothea had not left us long before another visitor as unexpected a one as her Ladyship, was announced. It was Sir Edward, who informed by Augusta of her Brother's marriage, came doubtless to reproach him for having dared to unite himself to me without his Knowledge. But Edward foreseeing his design, approached him with heroic fortitude as soon as he entered the Room, and addressed him in the following Manner.

"Sir Edward, I know the motive of your Journey here— You come with the base Design of reproaching me for having entered into an indissoluble engagement with my Laura without your Consent. But Sir, I glory in the Act—.

It is my greatest boast that I have incurred the displeasure of my Father!"

So saying, he took my hand and whilst Sir Edward, Philippa, and Augusta were doubtless reflecting with admiration on his undaunted Bravery, led me from the Parlour to his Father's Carriage which yet remained at the Door and in which we were instantly conveyed from the pursuit of Sir Edward.

The Postilions had at first received orders only to take the London road; as soon as we had sufficiently reflected However, we ordered them to Drive to M———. the seat of Edward's most particular freind, which was but a few miles distant.

At M———. we arrived in a few hours; and on sending in our names were immediately admitted to Sophia, the Wife of Edward's freind. After having been deprived during the course of 3 weeks of a real freind (for such I term your Mother) imagine my transports at beholding one, most truly worthy of the Name. Sophia was rather above the middle size; most elegantly formed. A soft languor spread over her lovely features, but increased their Beauty—. It was the Charectarestic of her Mind—. She was all sensibility and Feeling. We flew into each others arms and after having exchanged vows of mutual Freindship for the rest of our Lives, instantly unfolded to each other the most inward secrets of our Hearts—. We were interrupted in the delightfull Employment by the entrance of Augustus, (Edward's freind) who was just returned from a solitary ramble.

Never did I see such an affecting Scene as was the meeting of Edward and Augustus.

"My Life! my Soul!" (exclaimed the former) "My adorable angel!" (replied the latter) as they flew into each other's arms. It was too pathetic for the feelings of Sophia and myself—We fainted alternately on a sofa. Adeiu Laura.

LETTER the 9th From the same to the same

Towards the close of the day we received the following Letter from Philippa.

"Sir Edward is greatly incensed by your abrupt departure; he has taken back Augusta to Bedfordshire. Much as I wish to enjoy again your charming society, I cannot determine to snatch you from that, of such dear and deserving Freinds—When your Visit to them is terminated, I trust you will return to the arms of your" "Philippa."

We returned a suitable answer to this affectionate Note and after thanking her for her kind invitation assured her that we would certainly avail ourselves of it, whenever we might have no other place to go to. Tho' certainly nothing could to any reasonable Being, have appeared more satisfactory, than so gratefull a reply to her invitation, yet I know not how it was, but she was certainly capricious enough to be displeased with our behaviour and in a few weeks after, either to revenge our Conduct, or releive her own solitude, married a young and illiterate Fortune-hunter. This imprudent step (tho' we were sensible that it would probably deprive us of that fortune which Philippa had ever taught us to expect) could not on our own accounts, excite from our exalted minds a single sigh; yet fearfull lest it might prove a source of endless misery to the deluded Bride, our trembling Sensibility was greatly affected when we were first informed of the Event. The affectionate Entreaties of Augustus and Sophia that we would for ever consider their House as our Home, easily prevailed on us to determine never more to leave them, In the society of my Edward and this Amiable Pair, I passed the happiest moments of my Life; Our time was most delightfully spent, in mutual Protestations of Freindship, and in vows of unalterable Love, in which we were secure from being interrupted, by intruding and disagreable Visitors, as Augustus and Sophia had on their first Entrance in the Neighbourhood, taken due care to inform the surrounding Families, that as their happiness centered wholly in themselves, they wished for no other society. But alas! my Dear Marianne such Happiness as I then enjoyed was too perfect to be lasting. A most severe and unexpected Blow at once destroyed every sensation of Pleasure. Convinced as you must be from what I have already told you concerning Augustus and Sophia, that there never were a happier Couple, I need not I imagine, inform you that their union had been contrary to the inclinations of their Cruel and Mercenery Parents; who had vainly endeavoured with obstinate Perseverance to force them into a Marriage with those whom they had ever abhorred; but with a Heroic Fortitude worthy to be related and admired, they had both, constantly refused to submit to such despotic Power.

After having so nobly disentangled themselves from the shackles of Parental Authority, by a Clandestine Marriage, they were determined never to forfeit the good opinion they had gained in the World, in so doing, by accepting any proposals of reconciliation that might be offered them by their Fathers—to this farther tryal of their noble independance however they never were exposed.

They had been married but a few months when our visit to them commenced during which time they had been amply supported by a considerable sum of money which Augustus had gracefully purloined from his unworthy father's Escritoire, a few days before his union with Sophia.

By our arrival their Expenses were considerably encreased tho' their means for supplying them were then nearly exhausted. But they, Exalted Creatures! scorned to reflect a moment on their pecuniary Distresses and would have blushed at the idea of paying their Debts.—Alas! what was their Reward for such disinterested Behaviour! The beautifull Augustus was arrested and we were all undone. Such perfidious Treachery in the merciless perpetrators of the Deed will shock your gentle nature Dearest Marianne as much as it then affected the Delicate sensibility of Edward, Sophia, your Laura, and of Augustus himself. To compleat such unparalelled Barbarity we were informed that an Execution in the House would shortly take place. Ah! what could we do but what we did! We sighed and fainted on the sofa. Adeiu Laura.

LETTER 10th LAURA in continuation

When we were somewhat recovered from the overpowering Effusions of our grief, Edward desired that we would consider what was the most prudent step to be taken in our unhappy situation while he repaired to his imprisoned freind to lament over his misfortunes. We promised that we would, and he set forwards on his journey to Town. During his absence we faithfully complied with his Desire and after the most mature Deliberation, at length agreed that the best thing we could do was to leave the House; of which we every moment expected the officers of Justice to take possession. We waited therefore with the greatest impatience, for the return of Edward in order to impart to him the result of our Deliberations. But no Edward appeared. In vain did we count the tedious moments of his absence—in vain did we weep—in vain even did we sigh—no Edward returned—. This was too cruel, too unexpected a Blow to our Gentle Sensibility—we could not support it—we could only faint. At length collecting all the Resolution I was Mistress of, I arose and after packing up some necessary apparel for Sophia and myself, I dragged her to a Carriage I had ordered and we instantly set out for London. As the Habitation of Augustus was within twelve miles of Town, it was not long e'er we arrived there, and no sooner had we entered Holboun than letting down one of the Front Glasses I enquired of every decent-looking Person that we passed "If they had seen my Edward?"

But as we drove too rapidly to allow them to answer my repeated Enquiries, I gained little, or indeed, no information concerning him. "Where am I to drive?" said the Postilion. "To Newgate Gentle Youth (replied I), to see Augustus." "Oh! no, no, (exclaimed Sophia) I cannot go to Newgate; I shall not be able to support the sight of my Augustus in so cruel a confinement—my feelings are sufficiently shocked by the RECITAL, of his Distress, but to behold it will overpower my Sensibility." As I perfectly agreed with her in the Justice of her Sentiments the Postilion was instantly directed to return into the Country. You may perhaps have been somewhat surprised my Dearest Marianne, that in the Distress I then endured, destitute of any support, and unprovided with any Habitation, I should never once have remembered my Father and Mother or my paternal Cottage in the Vale of Uske. To account for this seeming forgetfullness I must inform you of a trifling circumstance concerning them which I have as yet never mentioned. The death of my Parents a few weeks after my Departure, is the circumstance I allude to. By their decease I became the lawfull Inheritress of their House and Fortune. But alas! the House had never been their own and their Fortune had only been an Annuity on their own Lives. Such is the Depravity of the World! To your Mother I should have returned with Pleasure, should have been happy to have introduced to her, my charming Sophia and should with Chearfullness have passed the remainder of my Life in their dear Society in the Vale of Uske, had not one obstacle to the execution of so agreable a scheme, intervened; which was the Marriage and Removal of your Mother to a distant part of Ireland. Adeiu Laura.

LETTER 11th LAURA in continuation

"I have a Relation in Scotland (said Sophia to me as we left London) who I am certain would not hesitate in receiving me." "Shall I order the Boy to drive there?" said I—but instantly recollecting myself, exclaimed, "Alas I fear it will be too long a Journey for the Horses." Unwilling however to act only from my own inadequate Knowledge of the Strength and Abilities of Horses, I consulted the Postilion, who was entirely of my Opinion concerning the Affair. We therefore determined to change Horses at the next Town and to travel Post the remainder of the Journey—. When we arrived at the last Inn we were to stop at, which was but a few miles from the House of Sophia's Relation, unwilling to intrude our Society on him unexpected and unthought of, we wrote a very elegant and well penned Note to him containing an account of our Destitute and melancholy Situation, and of our intention to spend some months with him in Scotland. As soon as we had dispatched this Letter, we immediately prepared to follow it in person and were stepping into the Carriage for that Purpose when our attention was attracted by the Entrance of a coroneted Coach and 4 into the Inn-yard. A Gentleman considerably advanced in years descended from it. At his first Appearance my Sensibility was wonderfully affected and e'er I had gazed at him a 2d time, an instinctive sympathy whispered to my Heart, that he was my Grandfather. Convinced that I could not be mistaken in my conjecture I instantly sprang from the Carriage I had just entered, and following the Venerable Stranger into the Room he had been shewn to, I threw myself on my knees before him and besought him to acknowledge me as his Grand Child. He started, and having attentively examined my features, raised me from the Ground and throwing his Grand-fatherly arms around my Neck, exclaimed, "Acknowledge thee! Yes dear resemblance of my Laurina and Laurina's Daughter, sweet image of my Claudia and my Claudia's Mother, I do acknowledge thee as the Daughter of the one and the Grandaughter of the other." While he was thus tenderly embracing me, Sophia astonished at my precipitate Departure, entered the Room in search of me. No sooner had she caught the eye of the venerable Peer, than he exclaimed with every mark of Astonishment—"Another Grandaughter! Yes, yes, I see you are the Daughter of my Laurina's eldest Girl; your resemblance to the beauteous Matilda sufficiently proclaims it. "Oh!" replied Sophia, "when I first beheld you the instinct of Nature whispered me that we were in some degree related—But whether Grandfathers, or Grandmothers, I could not pretend to determine." He folded her in his arms, and whilst they were tenderly embracing, the Door of the Apartment opened and a most beautifull young Man appeared. On perceiving him Lord St. Clair started and retreating back a few paces, with uplifted Hands, said, "Another Grand-child! What an unexpected Happiness is this! to discover in the space of 3 minutes, as many of my Descendants! This I am certain is Philander the son of my Laurina's 3d girl the amiable Bertha; there wants now but the presence of Gustavus to compleat the Union of my Laurina's Grand-Children."

"And here he is; (said a Gracefull Youth who that instant entered the room) here is the Gustavus you desire to see. I am the son of Agatha your Laurina's 4th and youngest Daughter," "I see you are indeed; replied Lord St. Clair— But tell me (continued he looking fearfully towards the

Door) tell me, have I any other Grand-children in the House." "None my Lord." "Then I will provide for you all without farther delay—Here are 4 Banknotes of 50L each—Take them and remember I have done the Duty of a Grandfather." He instantly left the Room and immediately afterwards the House. Adeiu, Laura.

LETTER the 12th LAURA in continuation

You may imagine how greatly we were surprised by the sudden departure of Lord St Clair. "Ignoble Grand-sire!" exclaimed Sophia. "Unworthy Grandfather!" said I, and instantly fainted in each other's arms. How long we remained in this situation I know not; but when we recovered we found ourselves alone, without either Gustavus, Philander, or the Banknotes. As we were deploring our unhappy fate, the Door of the Apartment opened and "Macdonald" was announced. He was Sophia's cousin. The haste with which he came to our releif so soon after the receipt of our Note, spoke so greatly in his favour that I hesitated not to pronounce him at first sight, a tender and simpathetic Freind. Alas! he little deserved the name— for though he told us that he was much concerned at our Misfortunes, yet by his own account it appeared that the perusal of them, had neither drawn from him a single sigh, nor induced him to bestow one curse on our vindic-tive stars—. He told Sophia that his Daughter depended on her returning with him to Macdonald-Hall, and that as his Cousin's freind he should be happy to see me there also. To

Macdonald-Hall, therefore we went, and were received with great kindness by Janetta the Daughter of Macdonald, and the Mistress of the Mansion. Janetta was then only fifteen; naturally well disposed, endowed with a susceptible Heart, and a simpathetic Disposition, she might, had these amiable qualities been properly encouraged, have been an ornament to human Nature; but unfortunately her Father possessed not a soul sufficiently exalted to admire so promising a Disposition, and had endeavoured by every means on his power to prevent it encreasing with her Years. He had actually so far extinguished the natural noble Sensibility of her Heart, as to prevail on her to accept an offer from a young Man of his Recommendation. They were to be married in a few months, and Graham, was in the House when we arrived. WE soon saw through his character. He was just such a Man as one might have expected to be the choice of Macdonald. They said he was Sensible, well-informed, and Agreable; we did not pretend to Judge of such trifles, but as we were convinced he had no soul, that he had never read the sorrows of Werter, and that his Hair bore not the least resemblance to auburn, we were certain that Janetta could feel no affection for him, or at least that she ought to feel none. The very circumstance of his being her father's choice too, was so much in his disfavour, that had he been deserving her, in every other respect yet THAT of itself ought to have been a sufficient reason in the Eyes of Janetta for rejecting him. These considerations we were determined to represent to her in their proper light and doubted not of meeting with the desired success from one naturally so well disposed; whose errors in the affair had only arisen from a want of proper confidence in her own opinion, and a suitable contempt of her father's. We found her indeed all that our warmest wishes could have hoped for; we had no difficulty to convince her that it was impossible she could love Graham, or that it was her Duty to disobey her Father; the only thing at which she rather seemed to hesitate was our assertion that she must be attached to some other Person. For some time, she persevered in declaring that she knew no other young man for whom she had the the smallest Affection; but upon explaining the impossibility of such a thing she said that she beleived she DID LIKE Captain M'Kenrie better than any one she knew besides. This confession satisfied us and after having enumerated the good Qualities of M'Kenrie and assured her that she was violently in love with him, we desired to know whether he had ever in any wise declared his affection to her.

"So far from having ever declared it, I have no reason to imagine that he has ever felt any for me." said Janetta. "That he certainly adores you (replied Sophia) there can be no doubt—. The Attachment must be reciprocal. Did he never gaze on you with admiration—tenderly press your hand—drop an involantary tear—and leave the room abruptly?" "Never (replied she) that I remember—he has always left the room indeed when his visit has been ended, but has never gone away particularly abruptly or without making a bow." Indeed my Love (said I) you must be mistaken—for it is absolutely impossible that he should ever have left you but with Confusion, Despair, and Precipitation. Consider but for a moment Janetta, and you must be convinced how absurd it is to suppose that he could ever make a Bow, or behave like any other Person." Having settled this Point to our satisfaction, the next we took into consideration was, to determine in what manner we should inform M'Kenrie of the favourable Opinion Janetta entertained of him.... We at length agreed to acquaint him with it by an anonymous Letter which Sophia drew up in the following manner.

"Oh! happy Lover of the beautifull Janetta, oh! amiable Possessor of HER Heart whose hand is destined to another, why do you thus delay a confession of your attachment to the amiable Object of it? Oh! consider that a few weeks will at once put an end to every flattering Hope that you may now entertain, by uniting the unfortunate Victim of her father's Cruelty to the execrable and detested Graham."

"Alas! why do you thus so cruelly connive at the projected Misery of her and of yourself by delaying to communicate that scheme which had doubtless long possessed your imagination? A secret Union will at once secure the felicity of both."

The amiable M'Kenrie, whose modesty as he afterwards assured us had been the only reason of his having so long concealed the violence of his affection for Janetta, on receiving this Billet flew on the wings of Love to Macdonald-Hall, and so powerfully pleaded his Attachment to her who inspired it, that after a few more private interveiws, Sophia and I experienced the satisfaction of seeing them depart for Gretna-Green, which they chose for the celebration of their Nuptials, in preference to any other place although it was at a considerable distance from Macdonald-Hall. Adeiu Laura.

LETTER the 13th LAURA in continuation

They had been gone nearly a couple of Hours, before either Macdonald or Graham had entertained any suspicion of the affair. And they might not even then have suspected it, but for the following little Accident. Sophia happening one day to open a private Drawer in Macdonald's Library with one of her own keys, discovered that it was the Place where he kept his Papers of consequence and amongst them some bank notes of considerable amount. This discovery she imparted to me; and having agreed together that it would be a proper treatment of so vile a Wretch as Macdonald to deprive him of money, perhaps dishonestly gained, it was determined that the next time we should either of us happen to go that way, we would take one or more of the Bank notes from the drawer. This well meant Plan we had often success-fully put in Execution; but alas! on the very day of Janetta's Escape, as Sophia was majestically removing the 5th Bank-note from the Drawer to her own purse, she was suddenly most impertinently interrupted in her employment by the entrance of Macdonald himself, in a most abrupt and pre-cipitate Manner. Sophia (who though naturally all winning sweetness could when occasions demanded it call forth the Dignity of her sex) instantly put on a most forbidding look, and darting an angry frown on the undaunted culprit, demanded in a haughty tone of voice "Wherefore her retire-ment was thus insolently broken in on?" The unblushing Macdonald, without even endeavouring to exculpate himself from the crime he was charged with, meanly endeavoured to reproach Sophia with ignobly defrauding him of his money . . . The dignity of Sophia was wounded; "Wretch (exclaimed she, hastily replacing the Bank-note in the Drawer) how darest thou to accuse me of an Act, of which the bare idea makes me blush?" The base wretch was still unconvinced and continued to upbraid the justly-offended Sophia in such opprobious Language, that at length he so greatly provoked the gentle sweetness of her Nature, as to induce her to revenge herself on him by informing him of Janetta's Elopement, and of the active Part we had both taken in the affair. At this period of their Quarrel I entered the Library and was as you may imagine equally offended as Sophia at the ill-grounded accusations of the malevolent and contemptible Macdonald. "Base Miscreant! (cried I) how canst thou thus undauntedly endeavour to sully the spotless reputation of such bright Excellence? Why dost thou not suspect MY innocence as soon?" "Be satisfied Madam (replied he) I DO suspect it, and therefore must desire that you will both leave this House in less than half an hour."

"We shall go willingly; (answered Sophia) our hearts have long detested thee, and nothing but our freindship for thy Daughter could have induced us to remain so long beneath thy roof."

"Your Freindship for my Daughter has indeed been most powerfully exerted by throwing her into the arms of an unprincipled Fortune-hunter." (replied he)

"Yes, (exclaimed I) amidst every misfortune, it will afford us some consolation to reflect that by this one act of Freindship to Janetta, we have amply discharged every obligation that we have received from her father."

"It must indeed be a most gratefull reflection, to your

exalted minds." (said he.)

As soon as we had packed up our wardrobe and valu-ables, we left Macdonald Hall, and after having walked about a mile and a half we sate down by the side of a clear limpid stream to refresh our exhausted limbs. The place was suited to meditation. A grove of full-grown Elms sheltered us from the East—. A Bed of full-grown Nettles from the West—. Before us ran the murmuring brook and behind us ran the turn-pike road. We were in a mood for contempla-tion and in a Disposition to enjoy so beautifull a spot. A mutual silence which had for some time reigned between us, was at length broke by my exclaiming—"What a lovely scene! Alas why are not Edward and Augustus here to enjoy its Beauties with us?"

"Ah! my beloved Laura (cried Sophia) for pity's sake forbear recalling to my remembrance the unhappy situation of my imprisoned Husband. Alas, what would I not give to learn the fate of my Augustus! to know if he is still in Newgate, or if he is yet hung. But never shall I be able so far to conquer my tender sensibility as to enquire after him. Oh! do not I beseech you ever let me again hear you repeat his beloved name—. It affects me too deeply—. I cannot bear to hear him mentioned it wounds my feelings."

"Excuse me my Sophia for having thus unwillingly offended you—" replied I—and then changing the con-versation, desired her to admire the noble Grandeur of the Elms which sheltered us from the Eastern Zephyr. "Alas! my Laura (returned she) avoid so melancholy a subject, I intreat you. Do not again wound my Sensibility by observa-tions on those elms. They remind me of Augustus. He was like them, tall, magestic—he possessed that noble grandeur which you admire in them."

I was silent, fearfull lest I might any more unwillingly distress her by fixing on any other subject of conversation which might again remind her of Augustus.

"Why do you not speak my Laura? (said she after a short pause) "I cannot support this silence you must not leave me to my own reflections; they ever recur to Augustus."

"What a beautifull sky! (said I) How charmingly is the azure varied by those delicate streaks of white!"

"Oh! my Laura (replied she hastily withdrawing her Eyes from a momentary glance at the sky) do not thus distress me by calling my Attention to an object which so cruelly reminds me of my Augustus's blue sattin waistcoat striped in white! In pity to your unhappy freind avoid a subject so distressing." What could I do? The feelings of Sophia were at that time so exquisite, and the tenderness she felt for Augustus so poignant that I had not power to start any other topic, justly fearing that it might in some unforseen manner again awaken all her sensibility by directing her thoughts to her Husband. Yet to be silent would be cruel; she had intreated me to talk.

From this Dilemma I was most fortunately releived by an accident truly apropos; it was the lucky overturning of a Gentleman's Phaeton, on the road which ran murmuring behind us. It was a most fortunate accident as it diverted the attention of Sophia from the melancholy reflections which she had been before indulging. We instantly quitted our seats and ran to the rescue of those who but a few moments before had been in so elevated a situation as a fashionably high

Phaeton, but who were now laid low and sprawling in the Dust. "What an ample subject for reflection on the uncertain Enjoyments of this World, would not that Phaeton and the Life of Cardinal Wolsey afford a thinking Mind!" said I to Sophia as we were hastening to the field of Action.

She had not time to answer me, for every thought was now engaged by the horrid spectacle before us. Two Gentlemen most elegantly attired but weltering in their blood was what first struck our Eyes—we approached—they were Edward and Augustus—. Yes dearest Marianne they were our Husbands. Sophia shreiked and fainted on the ground—I screamed and instantly ran mad—. We remained thus mutually deprived of our senses, some minutes, and on regaining them were deprived of them again. For an Hour and a Quarter did we continue in this unfortunate situation—Sophia fainting every moment and I running mad as often. At length a groan from the hapless Edward (who alone retained any share of life) restored us to ourselves. Had we indeed before imagined that either of them lived, we should have been more sparing of our Greif—but as we had supposed when we first beheld them that they were no more, we knew that nothing could remain to be done but what we were about. No sooner did we therefore hear my Edward's groan than postponing our lamentations for the present, we hastily ran to the Dear Youth and kneeling on each side of him implored him not to die—. "Laura (said He fixing his now languid Eyes on me) I fear I have been overturned."

I was overjoyed to find him yet sensible.

"Oh! tell me Edward (said I) tell me I beseech you before you die, what has befallen you since that unhappy Day in which Augustus was arrested and we were separated—"

"I will" (said he) and instantly fetching a deep sigh, Expired—. Sophia immediately sank again into a swoon—. MY grief was more audible. My Voice faltered, My Eyes assumed a vacant stare, my face became as pale as Death, and my senses were considerably impaired—.

"Talk not to me of Phaetons (said I, raving in a frantic, incoherent manner)—Give me a violin—. I'll play to him and sooth him in his melancholy Hours—Beware ye gentle Nymphs of Cupid's Thunderbolts, avoid the piercing shafts of Jupiter—Look at that grove of Firs—I see a Leg of Mutton—They told me Edward was not Dead; but they deceived me—they took him for a cucumber—" Thus I continued wildly exclaiming on my Edward's Death—. For two Hours did I rave thus madly and should not then have left off, as I was not in the least fatigued, had not Sophia who was just recovered from her swoon, intreated me to consider that Night was now approaching and that the Damps began to fall. "And whither shall we go (said I) to shelter us from either?" "To that white Cottage." (replied she pointing to a neat Building which rose up amidst the grove of Elms and which I had not before observed—) I agreed and we instantly walked to it—we knocked at the door—it was opened by an old woman; on being requested to afford us a Night's Lodging, she informed us that her House was but small, that she had only two Bedrooms, but that However we should be wellcome to one of them. We were satisfied and followed the good woman into the House where we were greatly cheered by the sight of a comfortable fire—. She was a widow and had only one Daughter, who was then just seventeen—One of the best of ages; but alas! she was very plain and her name was Bridget . . . Nothing therfore could be expected from her—she could not be supposed to possess either exalted Ideas, Delicate Feelings or refined Sensibilities—. She was nothing more than a mere good-tempered, civil and obliging young woman; as such we could scarcely dislike here—she was only an Object of Contempt—. Adeiu Laura.

LETTER the 14th LAURA in continuation

Arm yourself my amiable young Freind with all the philosophy you are Mistress of; summon up all the fortitude you possess, for alas! in the perusal of the following Pages your sensibility will be most severely tried. Ah! what were the misfortunes I had before experienced and which I have already related to you, to the one I am now going to inform you of. The Death of my Father and my Mother and my Husband though almost more than my gentle Nature could support, were trifles in comparison to the misfortune I am now proceeding to relate. The morning after our arrival at the Cottage, Sophia complained of a violent pain in her delicate limbs, accompanied with a disagreable Head-ake She attributed it to a cold caught by her continued faintings in the open air as the Dew was falling the Evening before. This I feared was but too probably the case; since how could it be otherwise accounted for that I should have escaped the same indisposition, but by supposing that the bodily Exertions I had undergone in my repeated fits of frenzy had so effectually circulated and warmed my Blood as to make me proof against the chilling Damps of Night, whereas, Sophia lying totally inactive on the ground must have been exposed to all their severity. I was most seriously alarmed by her illness which trifling as it may appear to you, a certain instinctive sensibility whispered me, would in the End be fatal to her.

Alas! my fears were but too fully justified; she grew gradually worse—and I daily became more alarmed for her. At length she was obliged to confine herself solely to the Bed allotted us by our worthy Landlady—. Her disorder turned to a galloping Consumption and in a few days carried her off. Amidst all my Lamentations for her (and violent you may suppose they were) I yet received some consolation in the reflection of my having paid every attention to her, that could be offered, in her illness. I had wept over her every Day—had bathed her sweet face with my tears and had pressed her fair Hands continually in mine—. "My beloved Laura (said she to me a few Hours before she died) take warning from my unhappy End and avoid the imprudent conduct which had occasioned it . . . Beware of fainting-fits . . . Though at the time they may be refreshing and agreable yet beleive me they will in the end, if too often repeated and at improper seasons, prove destructive to your Constitution . . . My fate will teach you this . . . I die a Martyr to my greif for the loss of Augustus . . . One fatal swoon has cost me my Life.. Beware of swoons Dear Laura . . . A frenzy fit is not one quarter so pernicious; it is an exercise to the Body and if not too violent, is I dare say conducive to Health in its consequences—Run mad as often as you chuse; but do not faint—"

These were the last words she ever addressed to me.. It was her dieing Advice to her afflicted Laura, who has ever most faithfully adhered to it.

After having attended my lamented freind to her Early Grave, I immediately (tho' late at night) left the detested Village in which she died, and near which had expired my Husband and Augustus. I had not walked many yards from it before I was overtaken by a stage-coach, in which I instantly took a place, determined to proceed in it to Edinburgh, where I hoped to find some kind some pitying Freind who would receive and comfort me in my afflictions.

It was so dark when I entered the Coach that I could not distinguish the Number of my Fellow-travellers; I could only perceive that they were many. Regardless however of anything concerning them, I gave myself up to my own sad Reflections. A general silence prevailed—A silence, which was by nothing interrupted but by the loud and repeated snores of one of the Party.

"What an illiterate villain must that man be! (thought I to myself) What a total want of delicate refinement must he have, who can thus shock our senses by such a brutal noise! He must I am certain be capable of every bad action! There is no crime too black for such a Character!" Thus reasoned I within myself, and doubtless such were the reflections of my fellow travellers.

At length, returning Day enabled me to behold the unprincipled Scoundrel who had so violently disturbed my feelings. It was Sir Edward the father of my Deceased Husband. By his side sate Augusta, and on the same seat with me were your Mother and Lady Dorothea. Imagine my surprise at finding myself thus seated amongst my old Acquaintance. Great as was my astonishment, it was yet increased, when on looking out of Windows, I beheld the Husband of Philippa, with Philippa by his side, on the Coachbox and when on looking behind I beheld, Philander and Gustavus in the Basket. "Oh! Heavens, (exclaimed I) is it possible that I should so unexpectedly be surrounded by my nearest Relations and Connections?" These words roused the rest of the Party, and every eye was directed to the corner in which I sat. "Oh! my Isabel (continued I throwing myself across Lady Dorothea into her arms) receive once more to your Bosom the unfortunate Laura. Alas! when we last parted in the Vale of Usk, I was happy in being united to the best of Edwards; I had then a Father and a Mother, and had never known misfortunes—But now deprived of every freind but you—"

"What! (interrupted Augusta) is my Brother dead then? Tell us I intreat you what is become of him?" "Yes, cold and insensible Nymph, (replied I) that luckless swain your Brother, is no more, and you may now glory in being the Heiress of Sir Edward's fortune."

Although I had always despised her from the Day I had overheard her conversation with my Edward, yet in civility I complied with hers and Sir Edward's intreaties that I would inform them of the whole melancholy affair. They were greatly shocked—even the obdurate Heart of Sir Edward and the insensible one of Augusta, were touched with sorrow, by the unhappy tale. At the request of your Mother I related to them every other misfortune which had befallen

me since we parted. Of the imprisonment of Augustus and
the absence of Edward—of our arrival in Scotland—of
our unexpected Meeting with our Grand-father and our
cousins—of our visit to Macdonald-Hall—of the singular
service we there performed towards Janetta—of her Fathers
ingratitude for it . . . of his inhuman Behaviour, unaccountable suspicions, and barbarous treatment of us, in obliging
us to leave the House . . . of our lamentations on the loss of
Edward and Augustus and finally of the melancholy Death
of my beloved Companion.

Pity and surprise were strongly depictured in your
Mother's countenance, during the whole of my narration,
but I am sorry to say, that to the eternal reproach of her
sensibility, the latter infinitely predominated. Nay, faultless
as my conduct had certainly been during the whole course
of my late misfortunes and adventures, she pretended to
find fault with my behaviour in many of the situations in
which I had been placed. As I was sensible myself, that I
had always behaved in a manner which reflected Honour
on my Feelings and Refinement, I paid little attention to
what she said, and desired her to satisfy my Curiosity by
informing me how she came there, instead of wounding my
spotless reputation with unjustifiable Reproaches. As soon
as she had complyed with my wishes in this particular and
had given me an accurate detail of every thing that had
befallen her since our separation (the particulars of which if
you are not already acquainted with, your Mother will give
you) I applied to Augusta for the same information respecting herself, Sir Edward and Lady Dorothea.

She told me that having a considerable taste for the

Beauties of Nature, her curiosity to behold the delightful scenes it exhibited in that part of the World had been
so much raised by Gilpin's Tour to the Highlands, that
she had prevailed on her Father to undertake a Tour to
Scotland and had persuaded Lady Dorothea to accompany
them. That they had arrived at Edinburgh a few Days
before and from thence had made daily Excursions into
the Country around in the Stage Coach they were then
in, from one of which Excursions they were at that time
returning. My next enquiries were concerning Philippa and
her Husband, the latter of whom I learned having spent all
her fortune, had recourse for subsistence to the talent in
which, he had always most excelled, namely, Driving, and
that having sold every thing which belonged to them except
their Coach, had converted it into a Stage and in order
to be removed from any of his former Acquaintance, had
driven it to Edinburgh from whence he went to Sterling
every other Day. That Philippa still retaining her affection
for her ungratefull Husband, had followed him to Scotland
and generally accompanied him in his little Excursions to
Sterling. "It has only been to throw a little money into their
Pockets (continued Augusta) that my Father has always
travelled in their Coach to veiw the beauties of the Country
since our arrival in Scotland—for it would certainly have
been much more agreable to us, to visit the Highlands in a
Postchaise than merely to travel from Edinburgh to Sterling
and from Sterling to Edinburgh every other Day in a
crowded and uncomfortable Stage." I perfectly agreed with
her in her sentiments on the affair, and secretly blamed Sir
Edward for thus sacrificing his Daughter's Pleasure for the

sake of a ridiculous old woman whose folly in marrying so young a man ought to be punished. His Behaviour however was entirely of a peice with his general Character; for what could be expected from a man who possessed not the smallest atom of Sensibility, who scarcely knew the meaning of simpathy, and who actually snored—. Adeiu Laura.

LETTER the 15th LAURA in continuation.

When we arrived at the town where we were to Breakfast, I was determined to speak with Philander and Gustavus, and to that purpose as soon as I left the Carriage, I went to the Basket and tenderly enquired after their Health, expressing my fears of the uneasiness of their situation. At first they seemed rather confused at my appearance dreading no doubt that I might call them to account for the money which our Grandfather had left me and which they had unjustly deprived me of, but finding that I mentioned nothing of the Matter, they desired me to step into the Basket as we might there converse with greater ease. Accordingly I entered and whilst the rest of the party were devouring green tea and buttered toast, we feasted ourselves in a more refined and sentimental Manner by a confidential Conversation. I informed them of every thing which had befallen me during the course of my life, and at my request they related to me every incident of theirs.

"We are the sons as you already know, of the two youngest Daughters which Lord St Clair had by Laurina an italian opera girl. Our mothers could neither of them

exactly ascertain who were our Father, though it is generally beleived that Philander, is the son of one Philip Jones
a Bricklayer and that my Father was one Gregory Staves
a Staymaker of Edinburgh. This is however of little consequence for as our Mothers were certainly never married
to either of them it reflects no Dishonour on our Blood,
which is of a most ancient and unpolluted kind. Bertha
(the Mother of Philander) and Agatha (my own Mother)
always lived together. They were neither of them very
rich; their united fortunes had originally amounted to
nine thousand Pounds, but as they had always lived on the
principal of it, when we were fifteen it was diminished to
nine Hundred. This nine Hundred they always kept in a
Drawer in one of the Tables which stood in our common
sitting Parlour, for the convenience of having it always at
Hand. Whether it was from this circumstance, of its being
easily taken, or from a wish of being independant, or from
an excess of sensibility (for which we were always remarkable) I cannot now determine, but certain it is that when
we had reached our 15th year, we took the nine Hundred
Pounds and ran away. Having obtained this prize we were
determined to manage it with eoconomy and not to spend it
either with folly or Extravagance. To this purpose we therefore divided it into nine parcels, one of which we devoted
to Victuals, the 2d to Drink, the 3d to Housekeeping, the
4th to Carriages, the 5th to Horses, the 6th to Servants,
the 7th to Amusements, the 8th to Cloathes and the 9th to
Silver Buckles. Having thus arranged our Expences for two
months (for we expected to make the nine Hundred Pounds
last as long) we hastened to London and had the good luck

to spend it in 7 weeks and a Day which was 6 Days sooner than we had intended. As soon as we had thus happily disencumbered ourselves from the weight of so much money, we began to think of returning to our Mothers, but accidentally hearing that they were both starved to Death, we gave over the design and determined to engage ourselves to some strolling Company of Players, as we had always a turn for the Stage. Accordingly we offered our services to one and were accepted; our Company was indeed rather small, as it consisted only of the Manager his wife and ourselves, but there were fewer to pay and the only inconvenience attending it was the Scarcity of Plays which for want of People to fill the Characters, we could perform. We did not mind trifles however—. One of our most admired Performances was MACBETH, in which we were truly great. The Manager always played BANQUO himself, his Wife my LADY MACBETH. I did the THREE WITCHES and Philander acted ALL THE REST. To say the truth this tragedy was not only the Best, but the only Play that we ever performed; and after having acted it all over England, and Wales, we came to Scotland to exhibit it over the remainder of Great Britain. We happened to be quartered in that very Town, where you came and met your Grandfather—. We were in the Inn-yard when his Carriage entered and perceiving by the arms to whom it belonged, and knowing that Lord St Clair was our Grandfather, we agreed to endeavour to get something from him by discovering the Relationship—. You know how well it succeeded—. Having obtained the two Hundred Pounds, we instantly left the Town, leaving our Manager and his

Wife to act MACBETH by themselves, and took the road to Sterling, where we spent our little fortune with great ECLAT. We are now returning to Edinburgh in order to get some preferment in the Acting way; and such my Dear Cousin is our History."

I thanked the amiable Youth for his entertaining narration, and after expressing my wishes for their Welfare and Happiness, left them in their little Habitation and returned to my other Freinds who impatiently expected me.

My adventures are now drawing to a close my dearest Marianne; at least for the present.

When we arrived at Edinburgh Sir Edward told me that as the Widow of his son, he desired I would accept from his Hands of four Hundred a year. I graciously promised that I would, but could not help observing that the unsimpathetic Baronet offered it more on account of my being the Widow of Edward than in being the refined and amiable Laura.

I took up my Residence in a Romantic Village in the Highlands of Scotland where I have ever since continued, and where I can uninterrupted by unmeaning Visits, indulge in a melancholy solitude, my unceasing Lamentations for the Death of my Father, my Mother, my Husband and my Freind.

Augusta has been for several years united to Graham the Man of all others most suited to her; she became acquainted with him during her stay in Scotland.

Sir Edward in hopes of gaining an Heir to his Title and Estate, at the same time married Lady Dorothea—. His wishes have been answered.

Philander and Gustavus, after having raised their

reputation by their Performances in the Theatrical Line at Edinburgh, removed to Covent Garden, where they still exhibit under the assumed names of LUVIS and QUICK.

Philippa has long paid the Debt of Nature, Her Husband however still continues to drive the Stage-Coach from Edinburgh to Sterling:—Adeiu my Dearest Marianne. Laura.

Finis

June 13th 1790.

AN UNFINISHED NOVEL IN LETTERS

To HENRY THOMAS AUSTEN Esqre.

Sir

I am now availing myself of the Liberty you have frequently honoured me with of dedicating one of my Novels to you. That it is unfinished, I greive; yet fear that from me, it will always remain so; that as far as it is carried, it should be so trifling and so unworthy of you, is another concern to your obliged humble Servant

The Author

Messrs Demand and Co—please to pay Jane Austen Spinster the sum of one hundred guineas on account of your Humble Servant.

H. T. Austen

L105. 0. 0.

LESLEY CASTLE

LETTER the FIRST is from Miss MARGARET LESLEY to Miss CHARLOTTE

LUTTERELL. Lesley Castle Janry 3rd—1792.

My Brother has just left us. "Matilda (said he at parting) you and Margaret will I am certain take all the care of my dear little one, that she might have received from an indulgent, and affectionate and amiable Mother." Tears rolled down his cheeks as he spoke these words—the remembrance of her, who had so wantonly disgraced the Maternal character and so openly violated the conjugal Duties, prevented his adding anything farther; he embraced his sweet Child and after saluting Matilda and Me hastily broke from us and seating himself in his Chaise, pursued the road to Aberdeen. Never was there a better young Man! Ah! how little did he deserve the misfortunes he has experienced in the Marriage state. So good a Husband to so bad a Wife! for you know my dear Charlotte that the Worthless Louisa left him, her Child and reputation a few weeks ago in company with Danvers and dishonour. Never was there a sweeter face, a finer form, or a less amiable Heart than Louisa owned! Her child already possesses the personal Charms of her unhappy Mother! May she inherit from her Father all his mental ones! Lesley is at present but five and twenty, and has already given himself up to melancholy and Despair; what a difference between him and his Father! Sir George is 57 and still remains the Beau, the flighty stripling, the gay Lad, and sprightly Youngster, that his Son was really about five years back, and that HE has affected to appear ever since my remembrance.

156

While our father is fluttering about the streets of London, gay, dissipated, and Thoughtless at the age of 57, Matilda and I continue secluded from Mankind in our old and Mouldering Castle, which is situated two miles from Perth on a bold projecting Rock, and commands an extensive veiw of the Town and its delightful Environs. But tho' retired from almost all the World, (for we visit no one but the M'Leods, The M'Kenzies, the M'Phersons, the M'Cartneys, the M'Donalds, The M'kinnons, the M'lellans, the M'kays, the Macbeths and the Macduffs) we are neither dull nor unhappy; on the contrary there never were two more lively, more agreable or more witty girls, than we are; not an hour in the Day hangs heavy on our Hands. We read, we work, we walk, and when fatigued with these Employments releive our spirits, either by a lively song, a graceful Dance, or by some smart bon-mot, and witty repartee. We are handsome my dear Charlotte, very handsome and the greatest of our Perfections is, that we are entirely insensible of them ourselves. But why do I thus dwell on myself! Let me rather repeat the praise of our dear little Neice the innocent Louisa, who is at present sweetly smiling in a gentle Nap, as she reposes on the sofa. The dear Creature is just turned of two years old; as handsome as tho' 2 and 20, as sensible as tho' 2 and 30, and as prudent as tho' 2 and 40. To convince you of this, I must inform you that she has a very fine complexion and very pretty features, that she already knows the two first letters in the Alphabet, and that she never tears her frocks—. If I have not now convinced you of her Beauty, Sense and Prudence, I have nothing more to urge in support of my assertion, and you will therefore have no way of deciding the Affair but by coming to Lesley-Castle, and by a personal acquaintance with Louisa, determine for yourself. Ah! my dear Freind, how happy should I be to see you within these venerable Walls! It is now four years since my removal from School has separated me from you; that two such tender Hearts, so closely linked together by the ties of simpathy and Freindship, should be so widely removed from each other, is vastly moving. I live in Perthshire, You in Sussex. We might meet in London, were my Father disposed to carry me there, and were your Mother to be there at the same time. We might meet at Bath, at Tunbridge, or anywhere else indeed, could we but be at the same place together. We have only to hope that such a period may arrive. My Father does not return to us till Autumn; my Brother will leave Scotland in a few Days; he is impatient to travel. Mistaken Youth! He vainly flatters himself that change of Air will heal the Wounds of a broken Heart! You will join with me I am certain my dear Charlotte, in prayers for the recovery of the unhappy Lesley's peace of Mind, which must ever be essential to that of your sincere freind M. Lesley.

LETTER the SECOND From Miss C. LUTTERELL to Miss M. LESLEY in answer.

Glenford Febry 12

I have a thousand excuses to beg for having so long delayed thanking you my dear Peggy for your agreable Letter, which beleive me I should not have deferred doing, had not every moment of my time during the last five weeks been so fully employed in the necessary arrangements for my sisters wedding, as to allow me no time to devote either to you or myself. And now what provokes me more than anything else is that the Match is broke off, and all my Labour thrown away. Imagine how great the Dissapointment must be to me, when you consider that after having laboured both by Night and by Day, in order to get the Wedding dinner ready by the time appointed, after having roasted Beef, Broiled Mutton, and Stewed Soup enough to last the new-married Couple through the Honey-moon, I had the mortification of finding that I had been Roasting, Broiling and Stewing both the Meat and Myself to no purpose. Indeed my dear Freind, I never remember suffering any vexation equal to what I experienced on last Monday when my sister came running to me in the store-room with her face as White as a Whipt syllabub, and told me that Hervey had been thrown from his Horse, had fractured his Scull and was pronounced by his surgeon to be in the most emminent Danger. "Good God! (said I) you dont say so? Why what in the name of Heaven will become of all the Victuals! We shall never be able to eat it while it is good. However, we'll call in the Surgeon to help us. I shall be able to manage the Sir-loin myself, my Mother will eat the soup, and You and the Doctor must finish the rest." Here I was interrupted, by seeing my poor Sister fall down to appearance Lifeless upon one of the Chests, where we keep our Table linen. I immediately called my Mother and the Maids, and at last we brought her to herself again; as soon as ever she was sensible, she expressed a determination of going instantly to Henry, and was so wildly bent on this Scheme, that we had the greatest Difficulty in the World to prevent her putting it in execution; at last however more by Force than Entreaty we prevailed on her to go into her room; we laid her upon the Bed, and she continued for some Hours in the most dreadful Convulsions. My Mother and I continued in the room with her, and when any intervals of tolerable Composure in Eloisa would allow us, we joined in heartfelt lamentations on the dreadful Waste in our provisions which this Event must occasion, and in concerting some plan for getting rid of them. We agreed that the best thing we could do was to begin eating them immediately, and accordingly we ordered up the cold Ham and Fowls, and instantly began our Devouring Plan on them with great Alacrity. We would have persuaded Eloisa to have taken a Wing of a Chicken, but she would not be persuaded. She was however much quieter than she had been; the convulsions she had before suffered having given way to an almost perfect Insensibility. We endeavoured to rouse her by every means in our power, but to no purpose. I talked to her of Henry. "Dear Eloisa (said I) there's no occasion for your crying so much about such a trifle. (for I was willing to make light of it in order to comfort her) I beg you would not mind it—You see it does not vex me in the least; though perhaps I may suffer most from it after all; for I shall not only be obliged to eat up all the Victuals I have dressed already, but must if Henry should recover (which however is not very likely) dress as much for you again; or should he die (as I suppose he will) I shall still have to prepare a Dinner for you whenever you marry any one else. So you see that tho' perhaps for the present it may afflict you to think of Henry's sufferings, Yet I dare say he'll die soon, and then his pain will be over and you will be easy, whereas my Trouble will last much longer for work as hard as I may, I am certain that the pantry cannot be cleared in less than a fortnight." Thus I did all in my power to console her, but without any effect, and at last as I saw that she did not seem to listen to me, I said no more, but leaving her with my Mother I took down the remains of The Ham and Chicken, and sent William to ask how Henry did. He was not expected to live many Hours; he died the same day. We took all possible care to break the melancholy Event to Eloisa in the tenderest manner; yet in spite of every precaution, her sufferings on hearing it were too violent for her reason, and she continued for many hours in a high Delirium. She is still extremely ill, and her Physicians are greatly afraid of her going into a Decline. We are therefore preparing for Bristol, where we mean to be in the course of the next week. And now my dear Margaret let me talk a little of your affairs; and in the first place I must inform you that it is confidently reported, your Father is going to be married; I am very unwilling to beleive so unpleasing a report, and at the same time cannot wholly discredit it. I have written to my freind Susan Fitzgerald, for information concerning it, which as she is at present in Town, she will be very able to give me. I know not who is the Lady. I think your Brother is extremely right in the resolution he has taken of travelling, as it will perhaps contribute to obliterate from his remembrance, those disagreable Events, which have lately so much afflicted him—I am happy to find that tho' secluded from all the World, neither you nor Matilda are dull or unhappy—that you may never know what it is to, be either is the wish of your sincerely affectionate C.L.

P. S. I have this instant received an answer from my freind Susan, which I enclose to you, and on which you will make your own reflections.

The enclosed LETTER

My dear CHARLOTTE You could not have applied for information concerning the report of Sir George Lesleys Marriage, to any one better able to give it you than I am. Sir George is certainly married; I was myself present at the Ceremony, which you will not be surprised at when I subscribe myself your Affectionate Susan Lesley

LETTER the THIRD From Miss MARGARET LESLEY to Miss C. LUTTERELL

Lesley Castle February the 16th

I have made my own reflections on the letter you enclosed to me, my Dear Charlotte and I will now tell you what those reflections were. I reflected that if by this second Marriage Sir George should have a second family, our fortunes must be considerably diminished—that if his Wife should be of an extravagant turn, she would encourage him to persevere in that gay and Dissipated way of Life to which little encouragement would be necessary, and which has I fear already proved but too detrimental to his health and fortune—that she would now become Mistress of those Jewels which once adorned our Mother, and which Sir George had always promised us—that if they did not come into Perthshire I should not be able to gratify my curiosity of beholding my Mother-in-law and that if they did, Matilda would no longer sit at the head of her Father's table—. These my dear Charlotte were the melancholy reflections which crowded into my imagination after perusing Susan's letter to you, and which instantly occurred to Matilda when she had perused it likewise. The same ideas, the same fears, immediately occupied her Mind, and I know not which reflection distressed her most, whether the probable Diminution of our Fortunes, or her own Consequence. We both wish very much to know whether Lady Lesley is handsome and what is your opinion of her; as you honour her with the appellation of your freind, we flatter ourselves that she must be amiable. My Brother is already in Paris. He intends to quit it in a few Days, and to begin his route to Italy. He writes in a most chearfull manner, says that the air of France has greatly recovered both his Health and Spirits; that he has now entirely ceased to think of Louisa with any degree either of Pity or Affection, that he even feels himself obliged to her for her Elopement, as he thinks it very good fun to be single again. By this, you may perceive that he has entirely regained that chearful Gaiety, and sprightly Wit, for which he was once so remarkable. When he first became acquainted with Louisa which was little more than three years ago, he was one of the most lively, the most agreable young Men of the age—. I beleive you never yet heard the particulars of his first acquaintance with her. It commenced at our cousin Colonel Drummond's; at whose house in Cumberland he spent the Christmas, in which he attained the age of two and twenty. Louisa Burton was the Daughter of a distant Relation of Mrs. Drummond, who dieing a few Months before in extreme poverty, left his only Child then about eighteen to the protection of any of his Relations who would protect her. Mrs. Drummond was the only one who found herself so disposed—Louisa was therefore removed from a miserable Cottage in Yorkshire to an elegant Mansion in Cumberland, and from every pecuniary Distress that Poverty could inflict, to every elegant Enjoyment that Money could purchase—. Louisa was naturally ill-tempered and Cunning; but she had been taught to disguise her real Disposition, under the appearance of insinuating Sweetness, by a father who but too well knew, that to be married, would be the only chance she would have of not being starved, and who flattered himself that with such an extroidinary share of personal beauty, joined to a gentleness of Manners, and an engaging address, she might stand a good chance of pleasing some young Man who might afford to marry a girl without a Shilling. Louisa perfectly entered into her father's schemes and was determined to forward them with all her care and attention. By dint of Perseverance and Application, she had at length so thoroughly disguised her natural disposition under the mask of Innocence, and Softness, as to impose upon every one who had not by a long and constant intimacy with her discovered her real Character. Such was Louisa when the hapless Lesley first beheld her at Drummond-house. His heart which (to use your favourite comparison) was as delicate as sweet and as tender as a Whipt-syllabub, could not resist her attractions. In a very few Days, he was falling in love, shortly after actually fell, and before he had known her a Month, he had married her. My Father was at first highly displeased at so hasty and imprudent a connection; but when he found that they did not mind it, he soon became perfectly reconciled to the match. The Estate near Aberdeen which my brother possesses by the bounty of his great Uncle independant of Sir George, was entirely sufficient to support him and my Sister in Elegance and Ease. For the first twelvemonth, no one could be happier than Lesley, and no one more amiable to appearance than Louisa, and so plausibly did she act and so cautiously behave that tho' Matilda and I often spent several weeks together with them, yet we neither of us had any suspicion of her real Disposition. After the birth of Louisa however, which one would have thought would have strengthened her regard for Lesley, the mask she had so long supported was by degrees thrown aside, and as probably she then thought herself secure in the affection of her Husband (which did indeed appear if possible augmented by the birth of his Child) she seemed to take no pains to prevent that affection from ever diminushing. Our visits therefore to Dunbeath, were now less frequent and by far less agreable than they used to be. Our absence was however never either mentioned or lamented by Louisa who in the society of young Danvers with whom she became acquainted at Aberdeen (he was at one of the Universities there,) felt infinitely happier than in that of Matilda and your freind, tho' there certainly never were pleasanter girls than we are. You know the sad end of all Lesleys connubial happiness; I will not repeat it—. Adeiu my dear Charlotte; although I have not yet mentioned anything of the matter, I hope you will do me the justice to beleive that I THINK and FEEL, a great deal for your Sisters affliction. I do not doubt but that the healthy air of the Bristol downs will intirely remove it, by erasing from her Mind the remembrance of Henry. I am my dear Charlotte yrs ever M. L.

LETTER the FOURTH From Miss C. LUTTERELL to Miss M. LESLEY

Bristol February 27th

My Dear Peggy I have but just received your letter, which being directed to Sussex while I was at Bristol was obliged to be forwarded to me here, and from some unaccountable Delay, has but this instant reached me—. I return you many thanks for the account it contains of Lesley's acquaintance, Love and Marriage with Louisa, which has not the less entertained me for having often been repeated to me before.

I have the satisfaction of informing you that we have every reason to imagine our pantry is by this time nearly cleared, as we left Particular orders with the servants to eat as hard as they possibly could, and to call in a couple of Chairwomen to assist them. We brought a cold Pigeon pye, a cold turkey, a cold tongue, and half a dozen Jellies with us, which we were lucky enough with the help of our Landlady, her husband, and their three children, to get rid of, in less than two days after our arrival. Poor Eloisa is still so very indifferent both in Health and Spirits, that I very much fear, the air of the Bristol downs, healthy as it is, has not been able to drive poor Henry from her remembrance.

You ask me whether your new Mother in law is handsome and amiable—I will now give you an exact description of her bodily and mental charms. She is short, and extremely well made; is naturally pale, but rouges a good deal; has fine eyes, and fine teeth, as she will take care to let you know as soon as she sees you, and is altogether very pretty. She is remarkably good-tempered when she has her own way, and very lively when she is not out of humour. She is naturally extravagant and not very affected; she never reads anything but the letters she receives from me, and never writes anything but her answers to them. She plays, sings and Dances, but has no taste for either, and excells in none, tho' she says she is passionately fond of all. Perhaps you may flatter me so far as to be surprised that one of whom I speak with so little affection should be my particular freind; but to tell you the truth, our freindship arose rather from Caprice on her side than Esteem on mine. We spent two or three days together with a Lady in Berkshire with whom we both happened to be connected—. During our visit, the Weather being remarkably bad, and our party particularly stupid, she was so good as to conceive a violent partiality for me, which very soon settled in a downright Freindship and ended in an established correspondence. She is probably by this time as tired of me, as I am of her; but as she is too Polite and I am too civil to say so, our letters are still as frequent and affectionate as ever, and our Attachment as firm and sincere as when it first commenced. As she had a great taste for the pleasures of London, and of Brighthelmstone, she will I dare say find some difficulty in prevailing on herself even to satisfy the curiosity I dare say she feels of beholding you, at the expence of quitting those favourite haunts of Dissipation, for the melancholy tho' venerable gloom of the castle you inhabit. Perhaps however if she finds her health impaired by too much amusement, she may acquire fortitude sufficient to undertake a Journey to Scotland in the hope of its Proving at least beneficial to her health, if not conducive to her happiness. Your fears I am sorry to say, concerning your father's extravagance, your own fortunes, your Mothers Jewels and your Sister's consequence, I should suppose are but too well founded. My freind herself has four thousand pounds, and will probably spend nearly as much every year in Dress and Public places, if she can get it—she will certainly not endeavour to reclaim Sir George from the manner of living to which he has been so long accustomed, and there is therefore some reason to fear that you will be very well off, if you get any fortune at all. The Jewels I should imagine too will undoubtedly be hers, and there is too much reason to think that she will preside at her Husbands table in preference to his Daughter. But as so melancholy a subject must necessarily extremely distress you, I will no longer dwell on it—.

Eloisa's indisposition has brought us to Bristol at so unfashionable a season of the year, that we have actually seen but one genteel family since we came. Mr and Mrs Marlowe are very agreable people; the ill health of their little boy occasioned their arrival here; you may imagine that being the only family with whom we can converse, we are of course on a footing of intimacy with them; we see them indeed almost every day, and dined with them yesterday. We spent a very pleasant Day, and had a very good Dinner, tho' to be sure the Veal was terribly under-done, and the Curry had no seasoning. I could not help wishing all dinner-time that I had been at the dressing it—. A brother of Mrs Marlowe, Mr Cleveland is with them at present; he is a good-looking young Man, and seems to have a good deal to say for himself. I tell Eloisa that she should set her cap at him, but she does not at all seem to relish the proposal. I should like to see the girl married and Cleveland has a very good estate. Perhaps you may wonder that I do not consider myself as well as my Sister in my matrimonial Projects; but to tell you the truth I never wish to act a more principal part at a Wedding than the superintending and directing the Dinner, and therefore while I can get any of my acquaintance to marry for me, I shall never think of doing it myself, as I very much suspect that I should not have so much time for dressing my own Wedding-dinner, as for dressing that of my freinds. Yours sincerely C. L.

LETTER the FIFTH Miss MARGARET LESLEY to Miss CHARLOTTE LUTTERELL

Lesley-Castle March 18th

On the same day that I received your last kind letter, Matilda received one from Sir George which was dated from Edinburgh, and informed us that he should do himself the pleasure of introducing Lady Lesley to us on the following evening. This as you may suppose considerably surprised us, particularly as your account of her Ladyship had given us reason to imagine there was little chance of her visiting Scotland at a time that London must be so gay. As it was our business however to be delighted at such a mark of condescension as a visit from Sir George and Lady Lesley, we prepared to return them an answer expressive of the happiness we enjoyed in expectation of such a Blessing, when luckily recollecting that as they were to reach the Castle the next Evening, it would be impossible for my father to receive it before he left Edinburgh, we contented ourselves with leaving them to suppose that we were as happy as we ought to be. At nine in the Evening on the following day, they came, accompanied by one of Lady Lesleys brothers. Her Ladyship perfectly answers the description you sent me of her, except that I do not think her so pretty as you seem to consider her. She has not a bad face, but there is something so extremely unmajestic in her little diminutive figure, as to render her in comparison with the elegant height of Matilda and Myself, an insignificant Dwarf. Her curiosity to see us (which must have been great to bring her

more than four hundred miles) being now perfectly gratified, she already begins to mention their return to town,
and has desired us to accompany her. We cannot refuse her
request since it is seconded by the commands of our Father,
and thirded by the entreaties of Mr. Fitzgerald who is certainly one of the most pleasing young Men, I ever beheld. It
is not yet determined when we are to go, but when ever we
do we shall certainly take our little Louisa with us. Adeiu
my dear Charlotte; Matilda unites in best wishes to you,
and Eloisa, with yours ever M. L.

LETTER the SIXTH LADY LESLEY to Miss CHARLOTTE LUTTERELL

Lesley-Castle March 20th

We arrived here my sweet Freind about a fortnight ago, and
I already heartily repent that I ever left our charming House
in Portman-square for such a dismal old weather-beaten
Castle as this. You can form no idea sufficiently hideous,
of its dungeon-like form. It is actually perched upon a
Rock to appearance so totally inaccessible, that I expected
to have been pulled up by a rope; and sincerely repented
having gratified my curiosity to behold my Daughters at the
expence of being obliged to enter their prison in so danger-
ous and ridiculous a manner. But as soon as I once found
myself safely arrived in the inside of this tremendous building, I comforted myself with the hope of having my spirits
revived, by the sight of two beautifull girls, such as the

Miss Lesleys had been represented to me, at Edinburgh. But here again, I met with nothing but Disappointment and Surprise. Matilda and Margaret Lesley are two great, tall, out of the way, over-grown, girls, just of a proper size to inhabit a Castle almost as large in comparison as themselves. I wish my dear Charlotte that you could but behold these Scotch giants; I am sure they would frighten you out of your wits. They will do very well as foils to myself, so I have invited them to accompany me to London where I hope to be in the course of a fortnight. Besides these two fair Damsels, I found a little humoured Brat here who I beleive is some relation to them, they told me who she was, and gave me a long rigmerole story of her father and a Miss SOMEBODY which I have entirely forgot. I hate scandal and detest Children. I have been plagued ever since I came here with tiresome visits from a parcel of Scotch wretches, with terrible hard-names; they were so civil, gave me so many invitations, and talked of coming again so soon, that I could not help affronting them. I suppose I shall not see them any more, and yet as a family party we are so stupid, that I do not know what to do with myself. These girls have no Music, but Scotch airs, no Drawings but Scotch Mountains, and no Books but Scotch Poems—and I hate everything Scotch. In general I can spend half the Day at my toilett with a great deal of pleasure, but why should I dress here, since there is not a creature in the House whom I have any wish to please. I have just had a conversation with my Brother in which he has greatly offended me, and which as I have nothing more entertaining to send you I will gave you the particulars of. You must know that I have for these 4 or 5 Days past strongly suspected William of entertaining a partiality to my eldest Daughter. I own indeed that had I been inclined to fall in love with any woman, I should not have made choice of Matilda Lesley for the object of my passion; for there is nothing I hate so much as a tall Woman: but however there is no accounting for some men's taste and as William is himself nearly six feet high, it is not wonderful that he should be partial to that height. Now as I have a very great affection for my Brother and should be extremely sorry to see him unhappy, which I suppose he means to be if he cannot marry Matilda, as moreover I know that his circumstances will not allow him to marry any one without a fortune, and that Matilda's is entirely dependant on her Father, who will neither have his own inclination nor my permission to give her anything at present, I thought it would be doing a good-natured action by my Brother to let him know as much, in order that he might choose for himself, whether to conquer his passion, or Love and Despair. Accordingly finding myself this Morning alone with him in one of the horrid old rooms of this Castle, I opened the cause to him in the following Manner.

"Well my dear William what do you think of these girls? for my part, I do not find them so plain as I expected: but perhaps you may think me partial to the Daughters of my Husband and perhaps you are right—They are indeed so very like Sir George that it is natural to think"—

"My Dear Susan (cried he in a tone of the greatest amazement) You do not really think they bear the least resemblance to their Father! He is so very plain!—but I beg your pardon—I had entirely forgotten to whom I was speaking—"

"Oh! pray dont mind me; (replied I) every one knows Sir George is horribly ugly, and I assure you I always thought him a fright."

"You surprise me extremely (answered William) by what you say both with respect to Sir George and his Daughters. You cannot think your Husband so deficient in personal Charms as you speak of, nor can you surely see any resemblance between him and the Miss Lesleys who are in my opinion perfectly unlike him and perfectly Handsome."

"If that is your opinion with regard to the girls it certainly is no proof of their Fathers beauty, for if they are perfectly unlike him and very handsome at the same time, it is natural to suppose that he is very plain."

"By no means, (said he) for what may be pretty in a Woman, may be very unpleasing in a Man."

"But you yourself (replied I) but a few minutes ago allowed him to be very plain."

"Men are no Judges of Beauty in their own Sex." (said he).

"Neither Men nor Women can think Sir George tolerable."

"Well, well, (said he) we will not dispute about HIS Beauty, but your opinion of his DAUGHTERS is surely very singular, for if I understood you right, you said you did not find them so plain as you expected to do!"

"Why, do YOU find them plainer then?" (said I).

"I can scarcely beleive you to be serious (returned he) when you speak of their persons in so extroidinary a

Manner. Do not you think the Miss Lesleys are two very handsome young Women?"

"Lord! No! (cried I) I think them terribly plain!"

"Plain! (replied He) My dear Susan, you cannot really think so! Why what single Feature in the face of either of them, can you possibly find fault with?"

"Oh! trust me for that; (replied I). Come I will begin with the eldest—with Matilda. Shall I, William?" (I looked as cunning as I could when I said it, in order to shame him).

"They are so much alike (said he) that I should suppose the faults of one, would be the faults of both."

"Well, then, in the first place; they are both so horribly tall!"

"They are TALLER than you are indeed." (said he with a saucy smile.)

"Nay, (said I), I know nothing of that."

"Well, but (he continued) tho' they may be above the common size, their figures are perfectly elegant; and as to their faces, their Eyes are beautifull."

"I never can think such tremendous, knock-me-down figures in the least degree elegant, and as for their eyes, they are so tall that I never could strain my neck enough to look at them."

"Nay, (replied he) I know not whether you may not be in the right in not attempting it, for perhaps they might dazzle you with their Lustre."

"Oh! Certainly. (said I, with the greatest complacency, for I assure you my dearest Charlotte I was not in the least offended tho' by what followed, one would suppose that William was conscious of having given me just cause to be so, for coming up to me and taking my hand, he said) "You must not look so grave Susan; you will make me fear I have offended you!"

"Offended me! Dear Brother, how came such a thought in your head! (returned I) No really! I assure you that I am not in the least surprised at your being so warm an advocate for the Beauty of these girls."—

"Well, but (interrupted William) remember that we have not yet concluded our dispute concerning them. What fault do you find with their complexion?"

"They are so horridly pale."

"They have always a little colour, and after any exercise it is considerably heightened."

"Yes, but if there should ever happen to be any rain in this part of the world, they will never be able raise more than their common stock—except indeed they amuse themselves with running up and Down these horrid old galleries and Antichambers."

"Well, (replied my Brother in a tone of vexation, and glancing an impertinent look at me) if they HAVE but little colour, at least, it is all their own."

This was too much my dear Charlotte, for I am certain that he had the impudence by that look, of pretending to suspect the reality of mine. But you I am sure will vindicate my character whenever you may hear it so cruelly aspersed, for you can witness how often I have protested against wearing Rouge, and how much I always told you I disliked it. And I assure you that my opinions are still the same.—. Well, not bearing to be so suspected by my Brother, I left the room immediately, and have been ever since in my own

Dressing-room writing to you. What a long letter have I made of it! But you must not expect to receive such from me when I get to Town; for it is only at Lesley castle, that one has time to write even to a Charlotte Lutterell.—. I was so much vexed by William's glance, that I could not summon Patience enough, to stay and give him that advice respecting his attachment to Matilda which had first induced me from pure Love to him to begin the conversation; and I am now so thoroughly convinced by it, of his violent passion for her, that I am certain he would never hear reason on the subject, and I shall there fore give myself no more trouble either about him or his favourite. Adeiu my dear girl—Yrs affectionately Susan L.

LETTER the SEVENTH From Miss C. LUTTERELL to Miss M. LESLEY

Bristol the 27th of March

I have received Letters from you and your Mother-in-law within this week which have greatly entertained me, as I find by them that you are both downright jealous of each others Beauty. It is very odd that two pretty Women tho' actually Mother and Daughter cannot be in the same House without falling out about their faces. Do be convinced that you are both perfectly handsome and say no more of the Matter. I suppose this letter must be directed to Portman Square where probably (great as is your affection for Lesley Castle) you will not be sorry to find yourself. In spite of all that people may say about Green fields and the Country I was always of opinion that London and its amusements must be very agreable for a while, and should be very happy could my Mother's income allow her to jockey us into its Public-places, during Winter. I always longed particularly to go to Vaux-hall, to see whether the cold Beef there is cut so thin as it is reported, for I have a sly suspicion that few people understand the art of cutting a slice of cold Beef so well as I do: nay it would be hard if I did not know something of the Matter, for it was a part of my Education that I took by far the most pains with. Mama always found me HER best scholar, tho' when Papa was alive Eloisa was HIS. Never to be sure were there two more different Dispositions in the World. We both loved Reading. SHE preferred Histories, and I Receipts. She loved drawing, Pictures, and I drawing Pullets. No one could sing a better song than she, and no one make a better Pye than I.—And so it has always continued since we have been no longer children. The only difference is that all disputes on the superior excellence of our Employments THEN so frequent are now no more. We have for many years entered into an agreement always to admire each other's works; I never fail listening to HER Music, and she is as constant in eating my pies. Such at least was the case till Henry Hervey made his appearance in Sussex. Before the arrival of his Aunt in our neighbourhood where she established herself you know about a twelvemonth ago, his visits to her had been at stated times, and of equal and settled Duration; but on her removal to the Hall which is within a walk from our House, they became both more frequent and longer. This as you may suppose could not be pleasing to Mrs Diana who is a professed enemy to everything which is not directed by Decorum and Formality, or which bears the least resemblance to Ease and Good-breeding. Nay so great was her aversion to her Nephews behaviour that I have often heard her give such hints of it before his face that had not Henry at such times been engaged in conversation with Eloisa, they must have caught his Attention and have very much distressed him. The alteration in my Sisters behaviour which I have before hinted at, now took place. The Agreement we had entered into of admiring each others productions she no longer seemed to regard, and tho' I constantly applauded even every Country-dance, she played, yet not even a pidgeon-pye of my making could obtain from her a single word of approbation. This was certainly enough to put any one in a Passion; however, I was as cool as a cream-cheese and having formed my plan and concerted a scheme of Revenge, I was determined to let her have her own way and not even to make her a single reproach. My scheme was to treat her as she treated me, and tho' she might even draw my own Picture or play Malbrook (which is the only tune I ever really liked) not to say so much as "Thank you Eloisa;" tho' I had for many years constantly hollowed whenever she played, BRAVO, BRAVISSIMO, ENCORE, DA CAPO, ALLEGRETTO, CON EXPRESSIONE, and POCO PRESTO with many other such outlandish words, all of them as Eloisa told me expressive of my Admiration; and so indeed I suppose they are, as I see some of them in every Page of every Music book, being the sentiments I imagine of the composer.

I executed my Plan with great Punctuality. I can not say success, for alas! my silence while she played seemed not in the least to displease her; on the contrary she actually said to me one day "Well Charlotte, I am very glad to find that you have at last left off that ridiculous custom of applauding my Execution on the Harpsichord till you made my head ake, and yourself hoarse. I feel very much obliged to you for keeping your admiration to yourself." I never shall forget the very witty answer I made to this speech. "Eloisa (said I) I beg you would be quite at your Ease with respect to all such fears in future, for be assured that I shall always keep my admiration to myself and my own pursuits and never extend it to yours." This was the only very severe thing I ever said in my Life; not but that I have often felt myself extremely satirical but it was the only time I ever made my feelings public.

I suppose there never were two Young people who had a greater affection for each other than Henry and Eloisa; no, the Love of your Brother for Miss Burton could not be so strong tho' it might be more violent. You may imagine therefore how provoked my Sister must have been to have him play her such a trick. Poor girl! she still laments his Death with undiminished constancy, notwithstanding he has been dead more than six weeks; but some People mind such things more than others. The ill state of Health into which his loss has thrown her makes her so weak, and so unable to support the least exertion, that she has been in tears all this Morning merely from having taken leave of Mrs. Marlowe who with her Husband, Brother and Child are to leave Bristol this morning. I am sorry to have them go because they are the only family with whom we have here any acquaintance, but I never thought of crying; to be sure Eloisa and Mrs Marlowe have always been more together than with me, and have therefore contracted a kind of affection for each other, which does not make Tears so inexcusable in them as they would be in me. The Marlowes are going to Town; Cliveland accompanies them; as neither Eloisa nor I could catch him I hope you or Matilda may have better Luck. I know not when we shall leave Bristol, Eloisa's spirits are so low that she is very averse to moving, and yet is certainly by no means mended by her residence here. A week or two will I hope determine our Measures— in the mean time believe me and etc—and etc—Charlotte Lutterell.

LETTER the EIGHTH Miss LUTTERELL to Mrs MARLOWE

Bristol April 4th

I feel myself greatly obliged to you my dear Emma for such a mark of your affection as I flatter myself was conveyed in the proposal you made me of our Corresponding; I assure you that it will be a great releif to me to write to you and as long as my Health and Spirits will allow me, you will find me a very constant correspondent; I will not say an entertaining one, for you know my situation suffciently not to be ignorant that in me Mirth would be improper and I know my own Heart too well not to be sensible that it would be unnatural. You must not expect news for we see no one with whom we are in the least acquainted, or in whose proceedings we have any Interest. You must not expect scandal for by the same rule we are equally debarred either from hearing or inventing it.—You must expect from me nothing but the melancholy effusions of a broken Heart which is ever reverting to the Happiness it once enjoyed and which ill supports its present wretchedness. The Possibility of being able to write, to speak, to you of my lost Henry will be a luxury to me, and your goodness will not I know refuse to read what it will so much releive my Heart to write. I once thought that to have what is in general called a Freind (I mean one of my own sex to whom I might speak with less reserve than to any other person) independant of my sister would never be an object of my wishes, but how much was I mistaken! Charlotte is too much engrossed by two confidential correspondents of that sort, to supply the place of one to me, and I hope you will not think me girlishly romantic, when I say that to have some kind and compassionate Freind who might listen to my sorrows without endeavouring to console me was what I had for some time wished for, when our acquaintance with you, the intimacy which followed it and the particular affectionate attention you paid me almost from the first, caused me to entertain the flattering Idea of those attentions being improved on a closer acquaintance into a Freindship which, if you were what my wishes formed you would be the greatest Happiness I could be capable of enjoying. To find that such Hopes are realised is a satisfaction indeed, a satisfaction which is now almost the only one I can ever experience.—I feel myself so languid that I am sure were you with me you would oblige me to leave off writing, and I cannot give you a greater proof of my affection for you than by acting, as I know you would wish me to do, whether Absent or Present. I am my dear Emmas sincere freind E. L.

LETTER the NINTH Mrs MARLOWE to Miss LUTTERELL

Grosvenor Street, April 10th

Need I say my dear Eloisa how wellcome your letter was to me I cannot give a greater proof of the pleasure I received from it, or of the Desire I feel that our Correspondence may be regular and frequent than by setting you so good an example as I now do in answering it before the end of the week—. But do not imagine that I claim any merit in being so punctual; on the contrary I assure you, that it is a far greater Gratification to me to write to you, than to spend the Evening either at a Concert or a Ball. Mr Marlowe is so desirous of my appearing at some of the Public places every evening that I do not like to refuse him, but at the same time so much wish to remain at Home, that inde-pendant of the Pleasure I experience in devoting any portion of my Time to my Dear Eloisa, yet the Liberty I claim from having a letter to write of spending an Evening at home with my little Boy, you know me well enough to be sensible, will of itself be a sufficient Inducement (if one is necessary) to my maintaining with Pleasure a Correspondence with you. As to the subject of your letters to me, whether grave or merry, if they concern you they must be equally interesting to me; not but that I think the melancholy Indulgence of your own sorrows by repeating them and dwelling on them to me, will only encourage and increase them, and that it will be more prudent in you to avoid so sad a subject; but yet knowing as I do what a soothing and melancholy Pleasure it must afford you, I cannot prevail on myself to deny you so great an Indulgence, and will only insist on your not expecting me to encourage you in it, by my own letters; on the contrary I intend to fill them with such lively Wit and enlivening Humour as shall even provoke a smile in the sweet but sorrowfull countenance of my Eloisa.

In the first place you are to learn that I have met your sisters three freinds Lady Lesley and her Daughters, twice in Public since I have been here. I know you will be impatient to hear my opinion of the Beauty of three Ladies of whom you have heard so much. Now, as you are too ill and too unhappy to be vain, I think I may venture to inform you that I like none of their faces so well as I do your own. Yet they are all handsome—Lady Lesley indeed I have seen before; her Daughters I beleive would in general be said to have a finer face than her Ladyship, and yet what with the charms of a Blooming complexion, a little Affectation and a great deal of small-talk, (in each of which she is superior to the young Ladies) she will I dare say gain herself as many admirers as the more regular features of Matilda, and Margaret. I am sure you will agree with me in saying that they can none of them be of a proper size for real Beauty, when you know that two of them are taller and the other shorter than ourselves. In spite of this Defect (or rather by reason of it) there is something very noble and majestic in the figures of the Miss Lesleys, and something agreably lively in the appearance of their pretty little Mother-in-law. But tho' one may be majestic and the other lively, yet the faces of neither possess that Bewitching sweetness of my Eloisas, which her present languor is so far from diminushing. What would my Husband and Brother say of us, if they knew all the fine things I have been saying to you in this letter. It is very hard that a pretty woman is never to be told she is so by any one of her own sex without that person's being suspected to be either her determined Enemy, or her professed Toad-eater. How much more amiable are women in that particular! One man may say forty civil things to another without our supposing that he is ever paid for it, and provided he does his Duty by our sex, we care not how Polite he is to his own.

Mrs Lutterell will be so good as to accept my compliments, Charlotte, my Love, and Eloisa the best wishes for the recovery of her Health and Spirits that can be offered by her affectionate Freind E. Marlowe.

I am afraid this letter will be but a poor specimen of my Powers in the witty way; and your opinion of them will not be greatly increased when I assure you that I have been as entertaining as I possibly could.

LETTER the TENTH From Miss MARGARET LESLEY to Miss CHARLOTTE LUTTERELL

Portman Square April 13th

MY DEAR CHARLOTTE We left Lesley-Castle on the 28th of last Month, and arrived safely in London after a Journey of seven Days; I had the pleasure of finding your Letter here waiting my Arrival, for which you have my grateful Thanks. Ah! my dear Freind I every day more regret the serene and tranquil Pleasures of the Castle we have left, in exchange for the uncertain and unequal Amusements of this vaunted City. Not that I will pretend to assert that these uncertain and unequal Amusements are in the least Degree unpleasing to me; on the contrary I enjoy them extremely and should enjoy them even more, were I not certain that every appearance I make in Public but rivetts the Chains of those unhappy Beings whose Passion it is impossible not to pity, tho' it is out of my power to return. In short my Dear Charlotte it is my sensibility for the sufferings of so many amiable young Men, my Dislike of the extreme admiration I meet with, and my aversion to being so celebrated both in Public, in Private, in Papers, and in Printshops, that are the reasons why I cannot more fully enjoy, the Amusements so various and pleasing of London. How often have I wished that I possessed as little Personal Beauty as you do; that my figure were as inelegant; my face as unlovely; and my appearance as unpleasing as yours! But ah! what little chance is there of so desirable an Event; I have had the small-pox, and must therefore submit to my unhappy fate.

I am now going to intrust you my dear Charlotte with a secret which has long disturbed the tranquility of my days, and which is of a kind to require the most inviolable Secrecy from you. Last Monday se'night Matilda and I accompanied Lady Lesley to a Rout at the Honourable Mrs Kickabout's; we were escorted by Mr Fitzgerald who is a very amiable young Man in the main, tho' perhaps a little singular in his Taste—He is in love with Matilda—. We had scarcely paid our Compliments to the Lady of the House and curtseyed to half a score different people when my Attention was attracted by the appearance of a Young Man the most lovely of his Sex, who at that moment entered the Room with another Gentleman and Lady. From the first moment I beheld him, I was certain that on him depended the future Happiness of my Life. Imagine my surprise when he was introduced to me by the name of Cleveland—I instantly recognised him as the Brother of Mrs Marlowe, and the acquaintance of my Charlotte at Bristol. Mr and Mrs M. were the gentleman and Lady who accompanied him. (You do not think Mrs Marlowe handsome?) The elegant address of Mr Cleveland, his polished Manners and Delightful Bow, at once confirmed my attachment. He did not speak; but I can imagine everything he would have said, had he opened his Mouth. I can picture to myself the cultivated Understanding, the Noble sentiments, and elegant Language which would have shone so conspicuous in the conversation of Mr Cleveland. The approach of Sir James Gower (one of my too numerous admirers) prevented the Discovery of any such Powers, by putting an end to a Conversation we had never commenced, and by attracting my attention to himself. But oh! how inferior are the accomplishments of Sir James to those of his so greatly envied Rival! Sir James is one of the most frequent of our Visitors, and is almost always of our Parties. We have since often met Mr and Mrs Marlowe but no Cleveland—he is always engaged some where else. Mrs Marlowe fatigues me to Death every time I see her by her tiresome Conversations about you and Eloisa. She is so stupid! I live in the hope of seeing her irrisistable Brother to night, as we are going to Lady Flambeaus, who is I know intimate with the Marlowes. Our party will be Lady Lesley, Matilda, Fitzgerald, Sir James Gower, and myself. We see little of Sir George, who is almost always at the gaming-table. Ah! my poor Fortune where art thou by this time? We see more of Lady L. who always makes her appearance (highly rouged) at Dinner-time. Alas! what Delightful Jewels will she be decked in this evening at Lady Flambeau's! Yet I wonder how she can herself delight in wearing them; surely she must be sensible of the ridiculous impropriety of loading her little diminutive figure with such superfluous ornaments; is it possible that she can not know how greatly superior an elegant simplicity is to the most studied apparel? Would she but Present them to Matilda and me, how greatly should we be obliged to her, How becoming would Diamonds be on our fine majestic figures! And how surprising it is that such an Idea should never have occurred to HER. I am sure if I have reflected in this manner once, I have fifty times. Whenever I see Lady Lesley dressed in them such reflections immediately come across me. My own Mother's Jewels too! But I will say no more on so melancholy a subject—let me entertain you with something more pleasing—Matilda had a letter this morning from Lesley, by which we have the pleasure of finding that he is at Naples has turned Roman-Catholic, obtained one of the Pope's Bulls for annulling his 1st Marriage and has since actually married a Neapolitan Lady of great Rank and Fortune. He tells us moreover that much the same sort of affair has befallen his first wife the worthless Louisa who is likewise at Naples had turned Roman-catholic, and is soon to be married to a Neapolitan Nobleman of great and Distinguished merit. He says, that they are at present very good Freinds, have quite forgiven all past errors and intend in future to be very good Neighbours. He invites Matilda and me to pay him a visit to Italy and to bring him his little Louisa whom both her Mother, Step-mother, and himself are equally desirous of beholding. As to our accepting his invitation, it is at Present very uncertain; Lady Lesley advises us to go without loss of time; Fitzgerald offers to escort us there, but Matilda has some doubts of the Propriety of such a scheme—she owns it would be very agreable. I am certain she likes the Fellow. My Father desires us not to be in a hurry, as perhaps if we wait a few months both he and Lady Lesley will do themselves the pleasure of attending us. Lady Lesley says no, that nothing will ever tempt her to forego the Amusements of Brighthelmstone for a Journey to Italy merely to see our Brother. "No (says the disagreable Woman) I have once in my life been fool enough to travel I dont know how many hundred Miles to see two of the Family, and I found it did not answer, so Deuce take me, if ever I am so foolish again." So says her Ladyship, but Sir George still Perseveres in saying that perhaps in a month or two, they may accompany us. Adeiu my Dear Charlotte Yrs faithful Margaret Lesley.

THE HISTORY OF ENGLAND

FROM THE REIGN OF HENRY THE 4TH TO THE DEATH OF CHARLES THE 1ST BY A PARTIAL, PREJUDICED, AND IGNORANT HISTORIAN.

To Miss Austen, eldest daughter of the Rev. George Austen, this work is inscribed with all due respect by THE AUTHOR.

N.B. There will be very few Dates in this History.

THE HISTORY OF ENGLAND

HENRY the 4th

Henry the 4th ascended the throne of England much to his own satisfaction in the year 1399, after having prevailed on his cousin and predecessor Richard the 2nd, to resign it to him, and to retire for the rest of his life to Pomfret Castle, where he happened to be murdered. It is to be supposed that Henry was married, since he had certainly four sons, but it is not in my power to inform the Reader who was his wife.

Be this as it may, he did not live for ever, but falling ill, his son the Prince of Wales came and took away the crown; whereupon the King made a long speech, for which I must refer the Reader to Shakespear's Plays, and the Prince made a still longer. Things being thus settled between them the King died, and was succeeded by his son Henry who had previously beat Sir William Gascoigne.

HENRY the 5th

This Prince after he succeeded to the throne grew quite reformed and amiable, forsaking all his dissipated companions, and never thrashing Sir William again. During his reign, Lord Cobham was burnt alive, but I forget what for. His Majesty then turned his thoughts to France, where he went and fought the famous Battle of Agincourt. He afterwards married the King's daughter Catherine, a very agreable woman by Shakespear's account. In spite of all this however he died, and was succeeded by his son Henry.

HENRY the 6th

I cannot say much for this Monarch's sense. Nor would I if I could, for he was a Lancastrian. I suppose you know all about the Wars between him and the Duke of York who was of the right side; if you do not, you had better read some other History, for I shall not be very diffuse in this, meaning by it only to vent my spleen AGAINST, and shew my Hatred TO all those people whose parties or principles do not suit with mine, and not to give information.

This King married Margaret of Anjou, a Woman whose distresses and misfortunes were so great as almost to make me who hate her, pity her. It was in this reign that Joan of Arc lived and made such a ROW among the English. They should not have burnt her—but they did. There were several Battles between the Yorkists and Lancastrians, in which the former (as they ought) usually conquered. At length they were entirely overcome; The King was murdered—The Queen was sent home—and Edward the 4th ascended the Throne.

EDWARD the 4th

This Monarch was famous only for his Beauty and his Courage, of which the Picture we have here given of him, and his undaunted Behaviour in marrying one Woman while he was engaged to another, are sufficient proofs. His Wife was Elizabeth Woodville, a Widow who, poor Woman! was afterwards confined in a Convent by that Monster of Iniquity and Avarice Henry the 7th. One of Edward's Mistresses was Jane Shore, who has had a play written about her, but it is a tragedy and therefore not worth reading. Having performed all these noble actions, his Majesty died, and was succeeded by his son.

EDWARD the 5th

This unfortunate Prince lived so little a while that nobody had him to draw his picture. He was murdered by his Uncle's Contrivance, whose name was Richard the 3rd.

RICHARD the 3rd

The Character of this Prince has been in general very severely treated by Historians, but as he was a YORK, I am rather inclined to suppose him a very respectable Man. It has indeed been confidently asserted that he killed his two Nephews and his Wife, but it has also been declared that he did not kill his two Nephews, which I am inclined to beleive true; and if this is the case, it may also be affirmed that he did not kill his Wife, for if Perkin Warbeck was really the Duke of York, why might not Lambert Simnel be the Widow of Richard. Whether innocent or guilty, he did not reign long in peace, for Henry Tudor E. of Richmond as great a villain as ever lived, made a great fuss about getting the Crown and having killed the King at the battle of Bosworth, he succeeded to it.

HENRY the 7th

This Monarch soon after his accession married the Princess Elizabeth of York, by which alliance he plainly proved that he thought his own right inferior to hers, tho' he pretended to the contrary. By this Marriage he had two sons and two daughters, the elder of which Daughters was married to the King of Scotland and had the happiness of being grandmother to one of the first Characters in the World. But of HER, I shall have occasion to speak more at large in future. The youngest, Mary, married first the King of France and secondly the D. of Suffolk, by whom she had one daughter, afterwards the Mother of Lady Jane

Grey, who tho' inferior to her lovely Cousin the Queen of Scots, was yet an amiable young woman and famous for reading Greek while other people were hunting. It was in the reign of Henry the 7th that Perkin Warbeck and Lambert Simnel before mentioned made their appearance, the former of whom was set in the stocks, took shelter in Beaulieu Abbey, and was beheaded with the Earl of Warwick, and the latter was taken into the Kings kitchen. His Majesty died and was succeeded by his son Henry whose only merit was his not being quite so bad as his daughter Elizabeth.

HENRY the 8th

It would be an affront to my Readers were I to suppose that they were not as well acquainted with the particulars of this King's reign as I am myself. It will therefore be saving THEM the task of reading again what they have read before, and MYSELF the trouble of writing what I do not perfectly recollect, by giving only a slight sketch of the principal Events which marked his reign. Among these may be ranked Cardinal Wolsey's telling the father Abbott of Leicester Abbey that "he was come to lay his bones among them," the reformation in Religion and the King's riding through the streets of London with Anna Bullen. It is however but Justice, and my Duty to declare that this amiable Woman was entirely innocent of the Crimes with which she was accused, and of which her Beauty, her Elegance, and her Sprightliness were sufficient proofs, not to mention her solemn Protestations of Innocence, the weakness of the Charges against her, and the King's Character; all of which add some confirmation, tho' perhaps but slight ones when in comparison with those before alledged in her favour. Tho' I do not profess giving many dates, yet as I think it proper to give some and shall of course make choice of those which it is most necessary for the Reader to know, I think it right to inform him that her letter to the King was dated on the 6th of May. The Crimes and Cruelties of this Prince, were too numerous to be mentioned, (as this history I trust has fully shown;) and nothing can be said in his vindication, but that his abolishing Religious Houses and leaving them to the ruinous depredations of time has been of infinite use to the landscape of England in general, which probably was a principal motive for his doing it, since otherwise why should a Man who was of no Religion himself be at so much trouble to abolish one which had for ages been established in the Kingdom. His Majesty's 5th Wife was the Duke of Norfolk's Neice who, tho' universally acquitted of the crimes for which she was beheaded, has been by many people supposed to have led an abandoned life before her Marriage—of this however I have many doubts, since she was a relation of that noble Duke of Norfolk who was so warm in the Queen of Scotland's cause, and who at last fell a victim to it. The Kings last wife contrived to survive him, but with difficulty effected it. He was succeeded by his only son Edward.

EDWARD the 6th

As this prince was only nine years old at the time of his Father's death, he was considered by many people as too young to govern, and the late King happening to be of the same opinion, his mother's Brother the Duke of Somerset was chosen Protector of the realm during his minority. This Man was on the whole of a very amiable Character, and is somewhat of a favourite with me, tho' I would by no means pretend to affirm that he was equal to those first of Men Robert Earl of Essex, Delamere, or Gilpin. He was beheaded, of which he might with reason have been proud, had he known that such was the death of Mary Queen of Scotland; but as it was impossible that he should be conscious of what had never happened, it does not appear that he felt particularly delighted with the manner of it. After his decease the Duke of Northumberland had the care of the King and the Kingdom, and performed his trust of both so well that the King died and the Kingdom was left to his daughter in law the Lady Jane Grey, who has been already mentioned as reading Greek. Whether she really understood that language or whether such a study proceeded only from an excess of vanity for which I beleive she was always rather remarkable, is uncertain. Whatever might be the cause, she preserved the same appearance of knowledge, and contempt of what was generally esteemed pleasure, during the whole of her life, for she declared herself displeased with being appointed Queen, and while conducting to the scaffold, she wrote a sentence in Latin and another in Greek on seeing the dead Body of her Husband accidentally passing that way.

MARY

This woman had the good luck of being advanced to the throne of England, in spite of the superior pretensions, Merit, and Beauty of her Cousins Mary Queen of Scotland and Jane Grey. Nor can I pity the Kingdom for the misfortunes they experienced during her Reign, since they fully deserved them, for having allowed her to succeed her Brother—which was a double peice of folly, since they might have foreseen that as she died without children, she would be succeeded by that disgrace to humanity, that pest of society, Elizabeth. Many were the people who fell martyrs to the protestant Religion during her reign; I suppose not fewer than a dozen. She married Philip King of Spain who in her sister's reign was famous for building Armadas. She died without issue, and then the dreadful moment came in which the destroyer of all comfort, the deceitful Betrayer of trust reposed in her, and the Murderess of her Cousin succeeded to the Throne.——

ELIZABETH

It was the peculiar misfortune of this Woman to have bad Ministers—-Since wicked as she herself was, she could not have committed such extensive mischeif, had not these vile and abandoned Men connived at, and encouraged her in her Crimes. I know that it has by many people been asserted and beleived that Lord Burleigh, Sir Francis Walsingham, and the rest of those who filled the cheif offices of State were deserving, experienced, and able Ministers. But oh!

how blinded such writers and such Readers must be to true Merit, to Merit despised, neglected and defamed, if they can persist in such opinions when they reflect that these men, these boasted men were such scandals to their Country and their sex as to allow and assist their Queen in confining for the space of nineteen years, a WOMAN who if the claims of Relationship and Merit were of no avail, yet as a Queen and as one who condescended to place confidence in her, had every reason to expect assistance and protection; and at length in allowing Elizabeth to bring this amiable Woman to an untimely, unmerited, and scandalous Death. Can any one if he reflects but for a moment on this blot, this everlasting blot upon their understanding and their Character, allow any praise to Lord Burleigh or Sir Francis Walsingham? Oh! what must this bewitching Princess whose only freind was then the Duke of Norfolk, and whose only ones now Mr Whitaker, Mrs Lefroy, Mrs Knight and myself, who was abandoned by her son, confined by her Cousin, abused, reproached and vilified by all, what must not her most noble mind have suffered when informed that Elizabeth had given orders for her Death! Yet she bore it with a most unshaken fortitude, firm in her mind; constant in her Religion; and prepared herself to meet the cruel fate to which she was doomed, with a magnanimity that would alone proceed from conscious Innocence. And yet could you Reader have beleived it possible that some hardened and zealous Protestants have even abused her for that steadfastness in the Catholic Religion which reflected on her so much credit? But this is a striking proof of THEIR narrow souls and prejudiced

Judgements who accuse her. She was executed in the Great Hall at Fortheringay Castle (sacred Place!) on Wednesday the 8th of February 1586—to the everlasting Reproach of Elizabeth, her Ministers, and of England in general. It may not be unnecessary before I entirely conclude my account of this ill-fated Queen, to observe that she had been accused of several crimes during the time of her reigning in Scotland, of which I now most seriously do assure my Reader that she was entirely innocent; having never been guilty of anything more than Imprudencies into which she was betrayed by the openness of her Heart, her Youth, and her Education. Having I trust by this assurance entirely done away every Suspicion and every doubt which might have arisen in the Reader's mind, from what other Historians have written of her, I shall proceed to mention the remaining Events that marked Elizabeth's reign. It was about this time that Sir Francis Drake the first English Navigator who sailed round the World, lived, to be the ornament of his Country and his profession. Yet great as he was, and justly celebrated as a sailor, I cannot help foreseeing that he will be equalled in this or the next Century by one who tho' now but young, already promises to answer all the ardent and sanguine expectations of his Relations and Freinds, amongst whom I may class the amiable Lady to whom this work is dedicated, and my no less amiable self.

Though of a different profession, and shining in a different sphere of Life, yet equally conspicuous in the Character of an Earl, as Drake was in that of a Sailor, was Robert Devereux Lord Essex. This unfortunate young Man was not unlike in character to that equally unfortunate one

FREDERIC DELAMERE. The simile may be carried still farther, and Elizabeth the torment of Essex may be compared to the Emmeline of Delamere. It would be endless to recount the misfortunes of this noble and gallant Earl. It is sufficient to say that he was beheaded on the 25th of Feb, after having been Lord Lieutenant of Ireland, after having clapped his hand on his sword, and after performing many other services to his Country. Elizabeth did not long survive his loss, and died so miserable that were it not an injury to the memory of Mary I should pity her.

JAMES the 1st

Though this King had some faults, among which and as the most principal, was his allowing his Mother's death, yet considered on the whole I cannot help liking him. He married Anne of Denmark, and had several Children; fortunately for him his eldest son Prince Henry died before his father or he might have experienced the evils which befell his unfortunate Brother.

As I am myself partial to the roman catholic religion, it is with infinite regret that I am obliged to blame the Behaviour of any Member of it: yet Truth being I think very excusable in an Historian, I am necessitated to say that in this reign the roman Catholics of England did not behave like Gentlemen to the protestants. Their Behaviour indeed to the Royal Family and both Houses of Parliament might justly be considered by them as very uncivil, and even Sir Henry Percy tho' certainly the best bred man of the party, had none of that general politeness which is so universally pleasing, as his attentions were entirely confined to Lord Mounteagle.

Sir Walter Raleigh flourished in this and the preceeding reign, and is by many people held in great veneration and respect—But as he was an enemy of the noble Essex, I have nothing to say in praise of him, and must refer all those who may wish to be acquainted with the particulars of his life, to Mr Sheridan's play of the Critic, where they will find many interesting anecdotes as well of him as of his friend Sir Christopher Hatton.—His Majesty was of that amiable disposition which inclines to Freindship, and in such points was possessed of a keener penetration in discovering Merit than many other people. I once heard an excellent Sharade on a Carpet, of which the subject I am now on reminds me, and as I think it may afford my Readers some amusement to FIND IT OUT, I shall here take the liberty of presenting it to them.

SHARADE My first is what my second was to King James the 1st, and you tread on my whole.

The principal favourites of his Majesty were Car, who was afterwards created Earl of Somerset and whose name perhaps may have some share in the above mentioned Sharade, and George Villiers afterwards Duke of Buckingham. On his Majesty's death he was succeeded by his son Charles.

CHARLES the 1st

This amiable Monarch seems born to have suffered misfortunes equal to those of his lovely Grandmother; misfortunes which he could not deserve since he was her descendant. Never certainly were there before so many detestable Characters at one time in England as in this Period of its History; never were amiable men so scarce. The number of them throughout the whole Kingdom amounting only to FIVE, besides the inhabitants of Oxford who were always loyal to their King and faithful to his interests. The names of this noble five who never forgot the duty of the subject, or swerved from their attachment to his Majesty, were as follows—The King himself, ever stedfast in his own support—Archbishop Laud, Earl of Strafford, Viscount Faulkland and Duke of Ormond, who were scarcely less strenuous or zealous in the cause. While the VILLIANS of the time would make too long a list to be written or read; I shall therefore content myself with mentioning the leaders of the Gang. Cromwell, Fairfax, Hampden, and Pym may be considered as the original Causers of all the disturbances, Distresses, and Civil Wars in which England for many years was embroiled. In this reign as well as in that of Elizabeth, I am obliged in spite of my attachment to the Scotch, to consider them as equally guilty with the generality of the English, since they dared to think differently from their Sovereign, to forget the Adoration which as STUARTS it was their Duty to pay them, to rebel against, dethrone and imprison the unfortunate Mary; to oppose, to deceive, and to sell the no less unfortunate Charles. The Events of this Monarch's reign are too numerous for my pen, and indeed the recital of any Events (except what I make myself) is uninteresting to me; my principal reason for undertaking the History of England being to Prove the innocence of the Queen of Scotland, which I flatter myself with having effectually done, and to abuse Elizabeth, tho' I am rather fearful of having fallen short in the latter part of my scheme.—As therefore it is not my intention to give any particular account of the distresses into which this King was involved through the misconduct and Cruelty of his Parliament, I shall satisfy myself with vindicating him from the Reproach of Arbitrary and tyrannical Government with which he has often been charged. This, I feel, is not difficult to be done, for with one argument I am certain of satisfying every sensible and well disposed person whose opinions have been properly guided by a good Education—and this Argument is that he was a STUART.

Finis Saturday Nov: 26th 1791.

A COLLECTION OF LETTERS

To Miss COOPER

COUSIN Conscious of the Charming Character which in every Country, and every Clime in Christendom is Cried, Concerning you, with Caution and Care I Commend to your Charitable Criticism this Clever Collection of Curious Comments, which have been Carefully Culled, Collected and Classed by your Comical Cousin

The Author.

A COLLECTION OF LETTERS

LETTER the FIRST From a MOTHER to her FREIND.

My Children begin now to claim all my attention in different Manner from that in which they have been used to receive it, as they are now arrived at that age when it is necessary for them in some measure to become conversant with the World, My Augusta is 17 and her sister scarcely a twelvemonth younger. I flatter myself that their education has been such as will not disgrace their appearance in the World, and that THEY will not disgrace their Education I have every reason to beleive. Indeed they are sweet Girls—. Sensible yet unaffected—Accomplished yet Easy—. Lively yet Gentle—. As their progress in every thing they have learnt has been always the same, I am willing to forget the difference of age, and to introduce them together into Public. This very Evening is fixed on as their first ENTREE into Life, as we are to drink tea with Mrs Cope and her Daughter. I am glad that we are to meet no one, for my Girls sake, as it would be awkward for them to enter too wide a Circle on the very first day. But we shall proceed by degrees.—Tomorrow Mr Stanly's family will drink tea with us, and perhaps the Miss Phillips's will meet them. On Tuesday we shall pay Morning Visits—On Wednesday we are to dine at Westbrook. On Thursday we have Company at home. On Friday we are to be at a Private Concert at Sir John Wynna's—and on Saturday we expect Miss Dawson to call in the Morning—which will complete my Daughters Introduction into Life. How they will bear so much dissipation I cannot imagine; of their spirits I have no fear, I only dread their health.

This mighty affair is now happily over, and my Girls are OUT. As the moment approached for our departure, you can have no idea how the sweet Creatures trembled with fear and expectation. Before the Carriage drove to the door, I called them into my dressing-room, and as soon as they were seated thus addressed them. "My dear Girls the moment is now arrived when I am to reap the rewards of all my Anxieties and Labours towards you during your Education. You are this Evening to enter a World in which you will meet with many wonderfull Things; Yet let me warn you against suffering yourselves to be meanly swayed by the Follies and Vices of others, for beleive me my beloved Children that if you do—I shall be very sorry for it." They both assured me that they would ever remember my advice with Gratitude, and follow it with attention; That they were prepared to find a World full of things to amaze and to shock them: but that they trusted their behaviour would never give me reason to repent the Watchful Care with which I had presided over their infancy and formed their Minds—" "With such expectations and such intentions (cried I) I can have nothing to fear from you—and can chearfully conduct you to Mrs Cope's without a fear of your being seduced by her Example, or contaminated by her Follies. Come, then my Children (added I) the Carriage is driving to the door, and I will not a moment delay the happiness you are so impatient to enjoy." When we arrived at Warleigh, poor Augusta could scarcely breathe, while Margaret was all Life and Rapture. "The long-expected Moment is now arrived (said she) and we shall soon be in the World."—In a few Moments we were in Mrs Cope's parlour, where with her daughter she sate ready to receive us. I observed with delight the impression my Children made on them—. They were indeed two sweet, elegant-looking Girls, and tho' somewhat abashed from the peculiarity of their situation, yet there was an ease in their Manners and address which could not fail of pleasing—. Imagine my dear Madam how delighted I must have been in beholding as I did, how attentively they observed every object they saw, how disgusted with some Things, how enchanted with others, how astonished at all! On the whole however they returned in raptures with the World, its Inhabitants, and Manners. Yrs Ever—A. F.

LETTER the SECOND From a YOUNG LADY crossed in Love to her freind

Why should this last disappointment hang so heavily on my spirits? Why should I feel it more, why should it wound me deeper than those I have experienced before? Can it be that I have a greater affection for Willoughby than I had for his amiable predecessors? Or is it that our feelings become more acute from being often wounded? I must suppose my dear Belle that this is the Case, since I am not conscious of being more sincerely attached to Willoughby than I was to Neville, Fitzowen, or either of the Crawfords, for all of whom I once felt the most lasting affection that ever warmed a Woman's heart. Tell me then dear Belle why I still sigh when I think of the faithless Edward, or why I weep when I behold his Bride, for too surely this is the case—. My Freinds are all alarmed for me; They fear my declining health; they lament my want of spirits; they dread the effects of both. In hopes of releiving my melancholy, by directing my thoughts to other objects, they have invited several of their freinds to spend the Christmas with us. Lady Bridget Darkwood and her sister-in-law, Miss Jane are expected on Friday; and Colonel Seaton's family will be with us next week. This is all most kindly meant by my Uncle and Cousins; but what can the presence of a dozen indefferent people do to me, but weary and distress me—. I will not finish my Letter till some of our Visitors are arrived.

Friday Evening Lady Bridget came this morning, and with her, her sweet sister Miss Jane—. Although I have been acquainted with this charming Woman above fifteen Years, yet I never before observed how lovely she is. She is now about 35, and in spite of sickness, sorrow and Time is more blooming than I ever saw a Girl of 17. I was delighted with her, the moment she entered the house, and she appeared equally pleased with me, attaching herself to me during the remainder of the day. There is something so sweet, so mild in her Countenance, that she seems more than Mortal. Her Conversation is as bewitching as her appearance; I could not help telling her how much she engaged my admiration—. "Oh! Miss Jane (said I)—and stopped from an inability at the moment of expressing myself as I could wish—Oh! Miss Jane—(I repeated)—I could not think of words to suit my feelings—She seemed waiting for my speech—. I was confused—distressed—my thoughts were bewildered—and I could only add—"How do you do?" She saw and felt for my Embarrassment and with admirable presence of mind releived me from it by saying—"My dear Sophia be not uneasy at having exposed yourself—I will turn the Conversation without appearing to notice it. "Oh! how I loved her for her kindness!" Do you ride as much as you used to do?" said she—. "I am advised to ride by my Physician. We have delightful Rides round us, I have a Charming horse, am uncommonly fond of the Amusement, replied I quite recovered from my Confusion, and in short I ride a great deal." "You are in the right my Love," said she. Then repeating the following line which was an extempore and equally adapted to recommend both Riding and Candour—

"Ride where you may, Be Candid where you can," she added," I rode once, but it is many years ago—She spoke this in so low and tremulous a Voice, that I was silent—. Struck with her Manner of speaking I could make no reply. "I have not ridden, continued she fixing her Eyes on my face, since I was married." I was never so surprised— "Married, Ma'am!" I repeated. "You may well wear that look of astonishment, said she, since what I have said must appear improbable to you—Yet nothing is more true than that I once was married."

"Then why are you called Miss Jane?"

"I married, my Sophia without the consent or knowledge of my father the late Admiral Annesley. It was therefore necessary to keep the secret from him and from every one, till some fortunate opportunity might offer of revealing it—. Such an opportunity alas! was but too soon given in the death of my dear Capt. Dashwood—Pardon these tears, continued Miss Jane wiping her Eyes, I owe them to my Husband's memory. He fell my Sophia, while fighting for his Country in America after a most happy Union of seven years—. My Children, two sweet Boys and a Girl, who had constantly resided with my Father and me, passing with him and with every one as the Children of a Brother (tho' I had ever been an only Child) had as yet been the comforts of my Life. But no sooner had I lossed my Henry, than these sweet Creatures fell sick and died—. Conceive dear Sophia what my feelings must have been when as an Aunt I attended my Children to their early Grave—. My Father did not survive them many weeks—He died, poor Good old man, happily ignorant to his last hour of my Marriage.'

"But did not you own it, and assume his name at your husband's death?"

"No; I could not bring myself to do it; more especially when in my Children I lost all inducement for doing it. Lady Bridget, and yourself are the only persons who are in the knowledge of my having ever been either Wife or Mother. As I could not Prevail on myself to take the name of Dashwood (a name which after my Henry's death I could never hear without emotion) and as I was conscious of having no right to that of Annesley, I dropt all thoughts of either, and have made it a point of bearing only my Christian one since my Father's death." She paused—"Oh! my dear Miss Jane (said I) how infinitely am I obliged to you for so entertaining a story! You cannot think how it has diverted me! But have you quite done?"

"I have only to add my dear Sophia, that my Henry's elder Brother dieing about the same time, Lady Bridget became a Widow like myself, and as we had always loved each other in idea from the high Character in which we had ever been spoken of, though we had never met, we determined to live together. We wrote to one another on the same subject by the same post, so exactly did our feeling and our actions coincide! We both eagerly embraced the proposals we gave and received of becoming one family, and have from that time lived together in the greatest affection."

"And is this all? said I, I hope you have not done."

"Indeed I have; and did you ever hear a story more pathetic?"

"I never did—and it is for that reason it pleases me so much, for when one is unhappy nothing is so delightful to one's sensations as to hear of equal misery."

"Ah! but my Sophia why are YOU unhappy?"

"Have you not heard Madam of Willoughby's Marriage?"

"But my love why lament HIS perfidy, when you bore so well that of many young Men before?"

"Ah! Madam, I was used to it then, but when Willoughby broke his Engagements I had not been dissapointed for half a year."

"Poor Girl!" said Miss Jane.

LETTER the THIRD From a YOUNG LADY in distressed Circumstances to her freind

A few days ago I was at a private Ball given by Mr Ashburnham. As my Mother never goes out she entrusted me to the care of Lady Greville who did me the honour of calling for me in her way and of allowing me to sit forwards, which is a favour about which I am very indifferent especially as I know it is considered as confering a great obligation on me "So Miss Maria (said her Ladyship as she saw me advancing to the door of the Carriage) you seem very smart to night—MY poor Girls will appear quite to disadvantage by YOU—I only hope your Mother may not have distressed herself to set YOU off. Have you got a new Gown on?"

"Yes Ma'am." replied I with as much indifference as I could assume.

"Aye, and a fine one too I think—(feeling it, as by her permission I seated myself by her) I dare say it is all very smart—But I must own, for you know I always speak my mind, that I think it was quite a needless piece of expence— Why could not you have worn your old striped one? It is not my way to find fault with People because they are poor, for I always think that they are more to be despised and pitied than blamed for it, especially if they cannot help it, but at the same time I must say that in my opinion your old striped Gown would have been quite fine enough for its Wearer—for to tell you the truth (I always speak my mind) I am very much afraid that one half of the people in the room will not know whether you have a Gown on or not— But I suppose you intend to make your fortune to night—. Well, the sooner the better; and I wish you success."

"Indeed Ma'am I have no such intention—"

"Who ever heard a young Lady own that she was a Fortune-hunter?" Miss Greville laughed but I am sure Ellen felt for me.

"Was your Mother gone to bed before you left her?" said her Ladyship.

"Dear Ma'am, said Ellen it is but nine o'clock."

"True Ellen, but Candles cost money, and Mrs Williams is too wise to be extravagant."

"She was just sitting down to supper Ma'am."

"And what had she got for supper?" "I did not observe." "Bread and Cheese I suppose." "I should never wish for a better supper." said Ellen. "You have never any reason replied her Mother, as a better is always provided for you." Miss Greville laughed excessively, as she constantly does at her Mother's wit.

Such is the humiliating Situation in which I am forced to appear while riding in her Ladyship's Coach—I dare not be impertinent, as my Mother is always admonishing me to be humble and patient if I wish to make my way in the world. She insists on my accepting every invitation of Lady Greville, or you may be certain that I would never enter either her House, or her Coach with the disagreable certainty I always have of being abused for my Poverty while I am in them.—When we arrived at Ashburnham, it was nearly ten o'clock, which was an hour and a half later than we were desired to be there; but Lady Greville is too fashionable (or fancies herself to be so) to be punctual. The Dancing however was not begun as they waited for Miss Greville. I had not been long in the room before I was engaged to dance by Mr Bernard, but just as we were going to stand up, he recollected that his Servant had got his white Gloves, and immediately ran out to fetch them. In the mean time the Dancing began and Lady Greville in passing to another room went exactly before me—She saw me and instantly stopping, said to me though there were several people close to us,

"Hey day, Miss Maria! What cannot you get a partner? Poor Young Lady! I am afraid your new Gown was put on for nothing. But do not despair; perhaps you may get a hop before the Evening is over." So saying, she passed on without hearing my repeated assurance of being engaged, and leaving me very much provoked at being so exposed before every one—Mr Bernard however soon returned and by coming to me the moment he entered the room, and leading me to the Dancers my Character I hope was cleared from the imputation Lady Greville had thrown on it, in the eyes of all the old Ladies who had heard her speech. I soon forgot all my vexations in the pleasure of dancing and of having the most agreable partner in the room. As he is moreover heir to a very large Estate I could see that Lady Greville did not look very well pleased when she found who had been his Choice—She was determined to mortify me, and accordingly when we were sitting down between the dances, she came to me with more than her usual insulting importance attended by Miss Mason and said loud enough to be heard by half the people in the room, "Pray Miss Maria in what way of business was your Grandfather? for Miss Mason and I cannot agree whether he was a Grocer or a Bookbinder." I saw that she wanted to mortify me, and was resolved if I possibly could to Prevent her seeing that her scheme succeeded. "Neither Madam; he was a Wine Merchant." "Aye, I knew he was in some such low way— He broke did not he?" "I beleive not Ma'am." "Did not he abscond?" "I never heard that he did." "At least he died insolvent?" "I was never told so before." "Why, was not your FATHER as poor as a Rat" "I fancy not." "Was not he in the Kings Bench once?" "I never saw him there." She gave me SUCH a look, and turned away in a great passion; while

I was half delighted with myself for my impertinence, and half afraid of being thought too saucy. As Lady Greville was extremely angry with me, she took no further notice of me all the Evening, and indeed had I been in favour I should have been equally neglected, as she was got into a Party of great folks and she never speaks to me when she can to anyone else. Miss Greville was with her Mother's party at supper, but Ellen preferred staying with the Bernards and me. We had a very pleasant Dance and as Lady G—slept all the way home, I had a very comfortable ride.

The next day while we were at dinner Lady Greville's Coach stopped at the door, for that is the time of day she generally contrives it should. She sent in a message by the servant to say that "she should not get out but that Miss Maria must come to the Coach-door, as she wanted to speak to her, and that she must make haste and come immediately—" "What an impertinent Message Mama!" said I—"Go Maria—" replied she—Accordingly I went and was obliged to stand there at her Ladyships pleasure though the Wind was extremely high and very cold.

"Why I think Miss Maria you are not quite so smart as you were last night—But I did not come to examine your dress, but to tell you that you may dine with us the day after tomorrow—Not tomorrow, remember, do not come tomorrow, for we expect Lord and Lady Clermont and Sir Thomas Stanley's family—There will be no occasion for your being very fine for I shant send the Carriage—If it rains you may take an umbrella—" I could hardly help laughing at hearing her give me leave to keep myself dry—"And pray remember to be in time, for I shant wait—I hate my Victuals over-done—But you need not come before the time—How does your Mother do? She is at dinner is not she?" "Yes Ma'am we were in the middle of dinner when your Ladyship came." "I am afraid you find it very cold Maria." said Ellen. "Yes, it is an horrible East wind—said her Mother—I assure you I can hardly bear the window down—But you are used to be blown about by the wind Miss Maria and that is what has made your Complexion so rudely and coarse. You young Ladies who cannot often ride in a Carriage never mind what weather you trudge in, or how the wind shews your legs. I would not have my Girls stand out of doors as you do in such a day as this. But some sort of people have no feelings either of cold or Delicacy—Well, remember that we shall expect you on Thursday at 5 o'clock—You must tell your Maid to come for you at night—There will be no Moon—and you will have an horrid walk home—My compts to Your Mother—I am afraid your dinner will be cold—Drive on—" And away she went, leaving me in a great passion with her as she always does. Maria Williams.

LETTER the FOURTH From a YOUNG LADY rather impertinent to her freind

We dined yesterday with Mr Evelyn where we were introduced to a very agreable looking Girl his Cousin. I was extremely pleased with her appearance, for added to the charms of an engaging face, her manner and voice had something peculiarly interesting in them. So much so, that they inspired me with a great curiosity to know the history of her Life, who were her Parents, where she came from, and what had befallen her, for it was then only known that she was a relation of Mr Evelyn, and that her name was Grenville. In the evening a favourable opportunity offered to me of attempting at least to know what I wished to know, for every one played at Cards but Mrs Evelyn, My Mother, Dr Drayton, Miss Grenville and myself, and as the two former were engaged in a whispering Conversation, and the Doctor fell asleep, we were of necessity obliged to entertain each other. This was what I wished and being determined not to remain in ignorance for want of asking, I began the Conversation in the following Manner.

"Have you been long in Essex Ma'am?"

"I arrived on Tuesday."

"You came from Derbyshire?"

"No, Ma'am! appearing surprised at my question, from Suffolk." You will think this a good dash of mine my dear Mary, but you know that I am not wanting for Impudence when I have any end in veiw. "Are you pleased with the Country Miss Grenville? Do you find it equal to the one you have left?"

"Much superior Ma'am in point of Beauty." She sighed. I longed to know for why.

"But the face of any Country however beautiful said I, can be but a poor consolation for the loss of one's dearest Freinds." She shook her head, as if she felt the truth of what I said. My Curiosity was so much raised, that I was resolved at any rate to satisfy it.

"You regret having left Suffolk then Miss Grenville?"
"Indeed I do." "You were born there I suppose?" "Yes

Ma'am I was and passed many happy years there—"

"That is a great comfort—said I—I hope Ma'am that you never spent any unhappy one's there."

"Perfect Felicity is not the property of Mortals, and no one has a right to expect uninterrupted Happiness.—Some Misfortunes I have certainly met with."

"WHAT Misfortunes dear Ma'am? replied I, burning with impatience to know every thing. "NONE Ma'am I hope that have been the effect of any wilfull fault in me." "I dare say not Ma'am, and have no doubt but that any sufferings you may have experienced could arise only from the cruelties of Relations or the Errors of Freinds." She sighed—" You seem unhappy my dear Miss Grenville—Is it in my power to soften your Misfortunes?" "YOUR power Ma'am replied she extremely surprised; it is in NO ONES power to make me happy." She pronounced these words in so mournfull and solemn an accent, that for some time I had not courage to reply. I was actually silenced. I recovered myself however in a few moments and looking at her with all the affection I could, "My dear Miss Grenville said I, you appear extremely young—and may probably stand in need of some one's advice whose regard for you, joined to superior Age, perhaps superior Judgement might authorise her to give it. I am that person, and I now challenge you to accept the offer I make you of my Confidence and Freindship, in return to which I shall only ask for yours—"

"You are extremely obliging Ma'am—said she—and I am highly flattered by your attention to me—But I am in no difficulty, no doubt, no uncertainty of situation in which any advice can be wanted. Whenever I am however continued she brightening into a complaisant smile, I shall know where to apply."

I bowed, but felt a good deal mortified by such a repulse; still however I had not given up my point. I found that by the appearance of sentiment and Freindship nothing was to be gained and determined therefore to renew my attacks by Questions and suppositions. "Do you intend staying long in this part of England Miss Grenville?"

"Yes Ma'am, some time I beleive."

"But how will Mr and Mrs Grenville bear your absence?"

"They are neither of them alive Ma'am." This was an answer I did not expect—I was quite silenced, and never felt so awkward in my Life—-.

LETTER the FIFTH From a YOUNG LADY very much in love to her Freind

My Uncle gets more stingy, my Aunt more particular, and I more in love every day. What shall we all be at this rate by the end of the year! I had this morning the happiness of receiving the following Letter from my dear Musgrove.

Sackville St: Janry 7th It is a month to day since I first beheld my lovely Henrietta, and the sacred anniversary must and shall be kept in a manner becoming the day—by writing to her. Never shall I forget the moment when her Beauties first broke on my sight—No time as you well know can erase it from my Memory. It was at Lady Scudamores.

Happy Lady Scudamore to live within a mile of the divine Henrietta! When the lovely Creature first entered the room, oh! what were my sensations? The sight of you was like the sight ofa wonderful fine Thing. I started—I gazed at her with admiration—She appeared every moment more Charming, and the unfortunate Musgrove became a captive to your Charms before I had time to look about me. Yes Madam, I had the happiness of adoring you, an happiness for which I cannot be too grateful. "What said he to himself is Musgrove allowed to die for Henrietta? Enviable Mortal! and may he pine for her who is the object of universal admiration, who is adored by a Colonel, and toasted by a Baronet! Adorable Henrietta how beautiful you are! I declare you are quite divine! You are more than Mortal. You are an Angel. You are Venus herself. In short Madam you are the prettiest Girl I ever saw in my Life—and her Beauty is encreased in her Musgroves Eyes, by permitting him to love her and allowing me to hope. And ah! Angelic Miss Henrietta Heaven is my witness how ardently I do hope for the death of your villanous Uncle and his abandoned Wife, since my fair one will not consent to be mine till their decease has placed her in affluence above what my fortune can procure—. Though it is an improvable Estate—. Cruel Henrietta to persist in such a resolution! I am at Present with my sister where I mean to continue till my own house which tho' an excellent one is at Present somewhat out of repair, is ready to receive me. Amiable princess of my Heart farewell—Of that Heart which trembles while it signs itself Your most ardent Admirer and devoted humble servt. T. Musgrove.

There is a pattern for a Love-letter Matilda! Did you ever read such a master-piece of Writing? Such sense, such sentiment, such purity of Thought, such flow of Language and such unfeigned Love in one sheet? No, never I can answer for it, since a Musgrove is not to be met with by every Girl. Oh! how I long to be with him! I intend to send him the following in answer to his Letter tomorrow.

My dearest Musgrove—. Words cannot express how happy your Letter made me; I thought I should have cried for joy, for I love you better than any body in the World. I think you the most amiable, and the handsomest Man in England, and so to be sure you are. I never read so sweet a Letter in my Life. Do write me another just like it, and tell me you are in love with me in every other line. I quite die to see you. How shall we manage to see one another? for we are so much in love that we cannot live asunder. Oh! my dear Musgrove you cannot think how impatiently I wait for the death of my Uncle and Aunt—If they will not Die soon, I beleive I shall run mad, for I get more in love with you every day of my Life.

How happy your Sister is to enjoy the pleasure of your Company in her house, and how happy every body in London must be because you are there. I hope you will be so kind as to write to me again soon, for I never read such sweet Letters as yours. I am my dearest Musgrove most truly and faithfully yours for ever and ever Henrietta Halton.

I hope he will like my answer; it is as good a one as I can write though nothing to his; Indeed I had always heard what a dab he was at a Love-letter. I saw him you know for the first time at Lady Scudamores—And when I saw her Ladyship afterwards she asked me how I liked her Cousin Musgrove?

"Why upon my word said I, I think he is a very handsome young Man."

"I am glad you think so replied she, for he is distractedly in love with you."

"Law! Lady Scudamore said I, how can you talk so ridiculously?"

"Nay, t'is very true answered she, I assure you, for he was in love with you from the first moment he beheld you."

"I wish it may be true said I, for that is the only kind of love I would give a farthing for—There is some sense in being in love at first sight."

"Well, I give you Joy of your conquest, replied Lady Scudamore, and I beleive it to have been a very complete one; I am sure it is not a contemptible one, for my Cousin is a charming young fellow, has seen a great deal of the World, and writes the best Love-letters I ever read."

This made me very happy, and I was excessively pleased with my conquest. However, I thought it was proper to give myself a few Airs—so I said to her—

"This is all very pretty Lady Scudamore, but you know that we young Ladies who are Heiresses must not throw ourselves away upon Men who have no fortune at all."

"My dear Miss Halton said she, I am as much convinced of that as you can be, and I do assure you that I should be the last person to encourage your marrying anyone who had not some pretensions to expect a fortune with you. Mr Musgrove is so far from being poor that he has an estate of several hundreds an year which is capable of great Improvement, and an excellent House, though at Present it is not quite in repair."

"If that is the case replied I, I have nothing more to say against him, and if as you say he is an informed young Man and can write a good Love-letter, I am sure I have no reason to find fault with him for admiring me, tho' perhaps I may not marry him for all that Lady Scudamore."

"You are certainly under no obligation to marry him answered her Ladyship, except that which love himself will dictate to you, for if I am not greatly mistaken you are at this very moment unknown to yourself, cherishing a most tender affection for him."

"Law, Lady Scudamore replied I blushing how can you think of such a thing?"

"Because every look, every word betrays it, answered she; Come my dear Henrietta, consider me as a freind, and be sincere with me—Do not you prefer Mr Musgrove to any man of your acquaintance?"

"Pray do not ask me such questions Lady Scudamore, said I turning away my head, for it is not fit for me to answer them."

"Nay my Love replied she, now you confirm my suspicions. But why Henrietta should you be ashamed to own a well-placed Love, or why refuse to confide in me?"

"I am not ashamed to own it; said I taking Courage. I do not refuse to confide in you or blush to say that I do love your cousin Mr Musgrove, that I am sincerely attached to him, for it is no disgrace to love a handsome Man. If he were plain indeed I might have had reason to be ashamed of a passion which must have been mean since the object would have been unworthy. But with such a figure and face, and such beautiful hair as your Cousin has, why should I blush to own that such superior merit has made an impression on me."

"My sweet Girl (said Lady Scudamore embracing me with great affection) what a delicate way of thinking you have in these matters, and what a quick discernment for one of your years! Oh! how I honour you for such Noble Sentiments!"

"Do you Ma'am said I; You are vastly obliging. But pray Lady Scudamore did your Cousin himself tell you of his affection for me I shall like him the better if he did, for what is a Lover without a Confidante?"

"Oh! my Love replied she, you were born for each other. Every word you say more deeply convinces me that your Minds are actuated by the invisible power of simpathy, for your opinions and sentiments so exactly coincide. Nay, the colour of your Hair is not very different. Yes my dear Girl, the poor despairing Musgrove did reveal to me the story of his Love—. Nor was I surprised at it—I know not how it was, but I had a kind of presentiment that he would be in love with you."

"Well, but how did he break it to you?"

"It was not till after supper. We were sitting round the fire together talking on indifferent subjects, though to say the truth the Conversation was cheifly on my side for he was thoughtful and silent, when on a sudden he interrupted me in the midst of something I was saying, by exclaiming in a most Theatrical tone—

Yes I'm in love I feel it now And Henrietta Halton has undone me

"Oh! What a sweet way replied I, of declaring his Passion! To make such a couple of charming lines about me! What a pity it is that they are not in rhime!"

"I am very glad you like it answered she; To be sure there was a great deal of Taste in it. And are you in love with her, Cousin? said I. I am very sorry for it, for unexceptionable as you are in every respect, with a pretty Estate capable of Great improvements, and an excellent House tho' somewhat out of repair, yet who can hope to aspire with success to the adorable Henrietta who has had an offer from a Colonel and been toasted by a Baronet"—"THAT I have—" cried I. Lady Scudamore continued. "Ah dear Cousin replied he, I am so well convinced of the little Chance I can have of winning her who is adored by thousands, that I need no assurances of yours to make me more thoroughly so. Yet surely neither you or the fair Henrietta herself will deny me the exquisite Gratification of dieing for her, of falling a victim to her Charms. And when I am dead"—continued her—

"Oh Lady Scudamore, said I wiping my eyes, that such a sweet Creature should talk of dieing!"

"It is an affecting Circumstance indeed, replied Lady Scudamore." "When I am dead said he, let me be carried and lain at her feet, and perhaps she may not disdain to drop a pitying tear on my poor remains."

"Dear Lady Scudamore interrupted I, say no more on this affecting subject. I cannot bear it."

"Oh! how I admire the sweet sensibility of your Soul,

and as I would not for Worlds wound it too deeply, I will be silent."

"Pray go on." said I. She did so.

"And then added he, Ah! Cousin imagine what my transports will be when I feel the dear precious drops trickle on my face! Who would not die to haste such extacy! And when I am interred, may the divine Henrietta bless some happier Youth with her affection, May he be as tenderly attached to her as the hapless Musgrove and while HE crumbles to dust, May they live an example of Felicity in the Conjugal state!"

Did you ever hear any thing so pathetic? What a charming wish, to be lain at my feet when he was dead! Oh! what an exalted mind he must have to be capable of such a wish! Lady Scudamore went on.

"Ah! my dear Cousin replied I to him, such noble behaviour as this, must melt the heart of any woman however obdurate it may naturally be; and could the divine Henrietta but hear your generous wishes for her happiness, all gentle as is her mind, I have not a doubt but that she would pity your affection and endeavour to return it." "Oh! Cousin answered he, do not endeavour to raise my hopes by such flattering assurances. No, I cannot hope to please this angel of a Woman, and the only thing which remains for me to do, is to die." "True Love is ever desponding replied I, but I my dear Tom will give you even greater hopes of conquering this fair one's heart, than I have yet given you, by assuring you that I watched her with the strictest attention during the whole day, and could plainly discover that she cherishes in her bosom though unknown to herself, a most tender affection for you."

"Dear Lady Scudamore cried I, This is more than I ever knew!"

"Did not I say that it was unknown to yourself? I did not, continued I to him, encourage you by saying this at first, that surprise might render the pleasure still Greater." "No Cousin replied he in a languid voice, nothing will convince me that I can have touched the heart of Henrietta Halton, and if you are deceived yourself, do not attempt deceiving me." "In short my Love it was the work of some hours for me to Persuade the poor despairing Youth that you had really a preference for him; but when at last he could no longer deny the force of my arguments, or discredit what I told him, his transports, his Raptures, his Extacies are beyond my power to describe."

"Oh! the dear Creature, cried I, how passionately he loves me! But dear Lady Scudamore did you tell him that I was totally dependant on my Uncle and Aunt?"

"Yes, I told him every thing."

"And what did he say."

"He exclaimed with virulence against Uncles and Aunts; Accused the laws of England for allowing them to Possess their Estates when wanted by their Nephews or Neices, and wished HE were in the House of Commons, that he might reform the Legislature, and rectify all its abuses."

"Oh! the sweet Man! What a spirit he has!" said I.

"He could not flatter himself he added, that the adorable Henrietta would condescend for his sake to resign those Luxuries and that splendor to which she had been used, and accept only in exchange the Comforts and Elegancies which his limited Income could afford her, even supposing that his house were in Readiness to receive her. I told him that it could not be expected that she would; it would be doing her an injustice to suppose her capable of giving up the power she now possesses and so nobly uses of doing such extensive Good to the poorer part of her fellow Creatures, merely for the gratification of you and herself."

"To be sure said I, I AM very Charitable every now and then. And what did Mr Musgrove say to this?"

"He replied that he was under a melancholy necessity of owning the truth of what I said, and that therefore if he should be the happy Creature destined to be the Husband of the Beautiful Henrietta he must bring himself to wait, however impatiently, for the fortunate day, when she might be freed from the power of worthless Relations and able to bestow herself on him."

What a noble Creature he is! Oh! Matilda what a fortunate one I am, who am to be his Wife! My Aunt is calling me to come and make the pies, so adeiu my dear freind, and beleive me yours etc—H. Halton.

Finis.

SCRAPS

To Miss FANNY CATHERINE AUSTEN

MY Dear Neice As I am prevented by the great distance between Rowling and Steventon from superintending your Education myself, the care of which will probably on that account devolve on your Father and Mother, I think it is my particular Duty to Prevent your feeling as much as possible the want of my personal instructions, by addressing to you on paper my Opinions and Admonitions on the conduct of Young Women, which you will find expressed in the following pages.—I am my dear Neice Your affectionate Aunt The Author.

THE FEMALE PHILOSOPHER

A LETTER

My Dear Louisa Your friend Mr Millar called upon us yesterday in his way to Bath, whither he is going for his health; two of his daughters were with him, but the eldest and the three Boys are with their Mother in Sussex. Though you have often told me that Miss Millar was remarkably handsome, you never mentioned anything of her Sisters' beauty; yet they are certainly extremely pretty. I'll give you their description.—Julia is eighteen; with a countenance in which Modesty, Sense and Dignity are happily blended, she has a form which at once presents you with Grace, Elegance and Symmetry. Charlotte who is just sixteen is shorter than her Sister, and though her figure cannot boast the easy dignity of Julia's, yet it has a pleasing plumpness which is in a different way as estimable. She is fair and her face is expressive sometimes of softness the most bewitching, and at others of Vivacity the most striking. She appears to have infinite Wit and a good humour unalterable; her conversation during the half hour they set with us, was replete with humourous sallies, Bonmots and repartees; while the sensible, the amiable Julia uttered sentiments of Morality worthy of a heart like her own. Mr Millar appeared to answer the character I had always received of him. My Father met him with that look of Love, that social Shake, and cordial kiss which marked his gladness at beholding an old and valued freind from whom thro' various circumstances he had been separated nearly twenty years. Mr Millar observed (and very justly too) that many events had befallen each during that interval of time, which gave occasion to the lovely Julia for making most sensible reflections on the many changes in their situation which so long a period had occasioned, on the advantages of some, and the disadvantages of others. From this subject she made a short digression to the instability of human pleasures and the uncertainty of their duration, which led her to observe that all earthly Joys must be imperfect. She was proceeding to illustrate this doctrine by examples from the Lives of great Men when the Carriage came to the Door and the amiable Moralist with her Father and Sister was obliged to depart; but not without a promise of spending five or six months with us on their return. We of course mentioned you, and I assure you that ample Justice was done to your Merits by all. "Louisa Clarke (said I) is in general a very pleasant Girl, yet sometimes her good humour is clouded by Peevishness, Envy and Spite. She neither wants Understanding or is without some pretensions to Beauty, but these are so very trifling, that the value she sets on her personal charms, and the adoration she expects them to be offered are at once a striking example of her vanity, her pride, and her folly." So said I, and to my opinion everyone added weight by the concurrence of their own. Your affectionate Arabella Smythe.

THE FIRST ACT OF A COMEDY

CHARACTERS Popgun Maria Charles Pistolletta
Postilion Hostess Chorus of ploughboys Cook and and
Strephon Chloe

SCENE—AN INN

ENTER Hostess, Charles, Maria, and Cook.

Hostess to Maria) If the gentry in the Lion should want
beds, shew them number 9.

Maria) Yes Mistress.—EXIT Maria

Hostess to Cook) If their Honours in the Moon ask for the
bill of fare, give it them.

Cook) I wull, I wull. EXIT Cook.

Hostess to Charles) If their Ladyships in the Sun ring their
Bell—answer it.

Charles) Yes Madam. EXEUNT Severally.

SCENE CHANGES TO THE MOON, and discovers
Popgun and Pistoletta.

Pistoletta) Pray papa how far is it to London?

Popgun) My Girl, my Darling, my favourite of all my Children, who art the picture of thy poor Mother who died two months ago, with whom I am going to Town to marry to Strephon, and to whom I mean to bequeath my whole Estate, it wants seven Miles.

SCENE CHANGES TO THE SUN—

ENTER Chloe and a chorus of ploughboys.

Chloe) Where am I? At Hounslow.—Where go I? To London—. What to do? To be married—. Unto whom? Unto Strephon. Who is he? A Youth. Then I will sing a song.

SONG I go to Town And when I come down, I shall be married to Streephon * [*Note the two e's] And that to me will be fun.

Chorus) Be fun, be fun, be fun, And that to me will be fun.

ENTER Cook—Cook) Here is the bill of fare.

Chloe reads) 2 Ducks, a leg of beef, a stinking partridge, and a tart.—I will have the leg of beef and the partridge.

EXIT Cook. And now I will sing another song.

SONG—I am going to have my dinner, After which I shan't be thinner, I wish I had here Strephon For he would carve the partridge if it should be a tough one.

Chorus) Tough one, tough one, tough one For he would carve the partridge if it Should be a tough one. EXIT Chloe and Chorus.—

SCENE CHANGES TO THE INSIDE OF THE LION.

Enter Strephon and Postilion. Streph:) You drove me from Staines to this place, from whence I mean to go to Town to marry Chloe. How much is your due?

Post:) Eighteen pence. Streph:) Alas, my freind, I have but a bad guinea with which I mean to support myself in Town. But I will pawn to you an undirected Letter that I received from Chloe.

Post:) Sir, I accept your offer.

END OF THE FIRST ACT.

A LETTER from a YOUNG LADY, whose feelings being too strong for her Judgement led her into the commission of Errors which her Heart disapproved.

Many have been the cares and vicissitudes of my past life, my beloved Ellinor, and the only consolation I feel for their bitterness is that on a close examination of my conduct, I am convinced that I have strictly deserved them. I murdered my father at a very early period of my Life, I have since murdered my Mother, and I am now going to murder my Sister. I have changed my religion so often that at present I have not an idea of any left. I have been a perjured witness in every public tryal for these last twelve years; and I have forged my own Will. In short there is scarcely a crime that I have not committed—But I am now going to reform.

Colonel Martin of the Horse guards has paid his Addresses to me, and we are to be married in a few days. As there is something singular in our Courtship, I will give you an account of it. Colonel Martin is the second son of the late Sir John Martin who died immensely rich, but bequeathing only one hundred thousand pound apeice to his three younger Children, left the bulk of his fortune, about eight Million to the present Sir Thomas. Upon his small pittance the Colonel lived tolerably contented for nearly four months when he took it into his head to determine on getting the whole of his eldest Brother's Estate. A new will was forged and the Colonel produced it in Court—but nobody would swear to it's being the right will except himself, and he had sworn so much that Nobody beleived him. At that moment I happened to be passing by the door of the Court, and was beckoned in by the Judge who told the Colonel that I was a Lady ready to witness anything for the cause of Justice, and advised him to apply to me. In short the Affair was soon adjusted. The Colonel and I swore to its' being the right will, and Sir Thomas has been obliged to resign all his ill-gotten wealth. The Colonel in gratitude waited on me the next day with an offer of his hand—. I am now going to murder my Sister. Yours Ever, Anna Parker.

A TOUR THROUGH WALES—in a LETTER from a YOUNG LADY—

My Dear Clara I have been so long on the ramble that I have not till now had it in my power to thank you for your

Letter—. We left our dear home on last Monday month; and proceeded on our tour through Wales, which is a principality contiguous to England and gives the title to the Prince of Wales. We travelled on horseback by preference. My Mother rode upon our little poney and Fanny and I walked by her side or rather ran, for my Mother is so fond of riding fast that she galloped all the way. You may be sure that we were in a fine perspiration when we came to our place of resting. Fanny has taken a great many Drawings of the Country, which are very beautiful, tho' perhaps not such exact resemblances as might be wished, from their being taken as she ran along. It would astonish you to see all the Shoes we wore out in our Tour. We determined to take a good Stock with us and therefore each took a pair of our own besides those we set off in. However we were obliged to have them both capped and heelpeiced at Carmarthen, and at last when they were quite gone, Mama was so kind as to lend us a pair of blue Sattin Slippers, of which we each took one and hopped home from Hereford delightfully—-I am your ever affectionate Elizabeth Johnson.

A TALE.

A Gentleman whose family name I shall conceal, bought a small Cottage in Pembrokeshire about two years ago. This daring Action was suggested to him by his elder Brother who promised to furnish two rooms and a Closet for him, provided he would take a small house near the borders of an extensive Forest, and about three Miles from the Sea.

Wilhelminus gladly accepted the offer and continued for some time searching after such a retreat when he was one morning agreably releived from his suspence by reading this advertisement in a Newspaper.

TO BE LETT A Neat Cottage on the borders of an extensive forest and about three Miles from the Sea. It is ready furnished except two rooms and a Closet.

The delighted Wilhelminus posted away immediately to his brother, and shewed him the advertisement. Robertus congratulated him and sent him in his Carriage to take possession of the Cottage. After travelling for three days and six nights without stopping, they arrived at the Forest and following a track which led by it's side down a steep Hill over which ten Rivulets meandered, they reached the Cottage in half an hour. Wilhelminus alighted, and after knocking for some time without receiving any answer or hearing any one stir within, he opened the door which was fastened only by a wooden latch and entered a small room, which he immediately perceived to be one of the two that were unfurnished—From thence he proceeded into a Closet equally bare. A pair of stairs that went out of it led him into a room above, no less destitute, and these apartments he found composed the whole of the House. He was by no means displeased with this discovery, as he had the comfort of reflecting that he should not be obliged to lay out any-thing on furniture himself—. He returned immediately to his Brother, who took him the next day to every Shop in Town, and bought what ever was requisite to furnish the two rooms and the Closet, In a few days everything was completed, and Wilhelminus returned to take possession of his Cottage. Robertus accompanied him, with his Lady the amiable Cecilia and her two lovely Sisters Arabella and Marina to whom Wilhelminus was tenderly attached, and a large number of Attendants.—An ordinary Genius might probably have been embarrassed, in endeavouring to accomodate so large a party, but Wilhelminus with admirable presence of mind gave orders for the immediate erection of two noble Tents in an open spot in the Forest adjoining to the house. Their Construction was both simple and elegant—A couple of old blankets, each supported by four sticks, gave a striking proof of that taste for architecture and that happy ease in overcoming difficulties which were some of Wilhelminus's most striking Virtues.